… Adam lifted one of the treats to his mouth. He closed his eyes as he took a bite, letting his head fall back on a decadent, throaty little moan. "Oh my God, dude, I could kiss you right now."

BEAUREGARD
AND THE BEAST

Evie Drae

Published by

 clandesdyne

Published by
CLANDESDYNE
PO Box 621
Barberton, OH 44203-0521
www.clandesdyne.com

Paperback ISBN: 978-1-952695-00-1
Digital ISBN: 978-1-952695-01-8
Library of Congress Control Number: 2020907479
Paperback published April 24, 2020
v. 2.0

To my husband, Benjamin, and our fur baby, Bacchus. Without your endless love, support, and patience, I couldn't do what I do.

Acknowledgments

The journey from a wannabe writer to a published novelist is a long and arduous one. They say it takes a village to raise a child, but it takes nearly as many to nurture an author. I'd like to extend all the "thank-yous" and send a million hugs, kisses, and chocolate to the following:

First, to Benjamin, the best life partner anyone could ever ask for, who puts my dreams at the top of our to-do list and endures my writing-induced tantrums with grace and civility. To my mother, who instilled the love of reading into me at a very young age. To my father and stepmother, who never fail to ask about and root for my writerly triumphs. To my brother Andy and his wife and daughter, Shaila and Ava, who will undoubtedly be among my first sales, even though Ava won't be allowed to read this story until she's at least eighteen. To my whole in-law clan, who love me as if I were a blooded daughter, sister, and aunt. To my Dollface, who always believes in me even when my self-doubt is at its highest. To Becky, who takes the love and devotion of a "twin sister" to a whole new level.

To my first-ever editor, Sione Aeschliman, who taught me the value of professional feedback and how to make my words sparkle. To my developmental editor Sue Brown-Moore, who saw potential in my voice and made my writerly dreams come true. To my senior editor, Desi Chapman, and all the rest of the amazing editorial staff, who helped make my words the best they could be.

To my incredible Twitter #amwriting community—most especially my #writeLGBTQ+ lovelies—who hold me up and keep me going, day in and day out. To my CPs/betas/writing cheerleaders—Jess, Hannah, Meka, Marit, Lindsay, Sarah, Courtney, Brent, Scott, Maureen, Cora, Tara, Julie, Alex, Jenn, Tia, J, Heather, Karen, and Micah—you're all gods and goddesses in my world. To my biggest supporters in this project, Laz and

Kristina, whose verbal pom-poms made this book possible. And finally, to my alpha reader and BFF, Lily, who holds the distinctive honor of being the first person to ever read my non-academic words. Without her encouragement, love, and late-night pep talks, I wouldn't be here today.

BEAUREGARD AND THE BEAST

AN MM ROMANCE FAIRY TALE RETELLING

Chapter One

Even in the air-conditioned interior of Adam's sprawling desert estate, the Las Vegas sun was oppressive. Late afternoon rays slanted through the blinds. They fell in even bands across the dove gray leather of the sofa, heating his bare skin.

He'd definitely made the right decision to forgo anything more than boxer briefs for his Sunday laze.

When the doorbell echoed through the two-story, open-concept living space, he frowned. Pushing to an elbow, he shut off the Raiders game. The chime sounded again, this time ringing out three times in quick succession. He chuckled. Only one person pounded on his bell with such ferocious impatience.

Kyle Bryant, his manager and longtime friend.

After bouncing to his feet, Adam hustled to the front door and threw it open. The grin splitting his face sank into a scowl. Kyle wasn't alone.

Shorter than Adam's six-foot-three-inch height by a

solid half foot, Kyle was still taller than the man beside him, who couldn't be more than five and a half feet tall and a buck-thirty soaking wet.

"You forgot, didn't you?" Kyle rolled his eyes, gave Adam's shoulder a shove, then barreled through the door. "If I go out of my way to play errand boy, the least you can do is make a note somewhere. Put a stickie on your goddamn mirror. Something."

Adam squinted an eye and glanced from Kyle, who'd made his way into the kitchen and had his ass in the air as he rummaged through the refrigerator, to the man still standing on his front porch. What had he forgotten? It was Sunday. His one day of semirest. Why would he agree to whatever the hell this was?

A pink flush colored the new guy's cheeks as he shifted from one foot to the other. Gorgeous green eyes bugged behind a pair of vintage browline glasses. He clutched an overstuffed duffel bag against his chest, and a large suitcase sat at his feet.

It was the luggage that finally flipped Adam's mental switch. Kyle had mentioned something earlier in the week about receiving a recommendation for someone to take over as his new personal assistant. He'd been without a PA for a couple of weeks now, after his last one got engaged and fled Sin City in favor of finding a place better suited to raising a family. Hiring a new one hadn't topped Adam's priority list—mostly because few things did unless they were related to his training—but Kyle didn't favor letting the position sit vacant for long.

Admittedly, Adam was forgetful on a good day and downright obtuse on his worst. Without someone else in his life to keep his schedule and maintain the bare necessities of his existence, he became an albatross around Kyle's neck. Which explained the luggage-wielding stranger on Adam's porch.

To save his own sanity, Kyle had taken it upon himself to locate and hire a replacement. Adam had declined any interest in the selection or interview process. He trusted Kyle's instincts, and if Kyle deemed this awkward young man worthy enough to keep his ass in line, he would too.

Kyle resurfaced with a Styrofoam to-go box in one hand and a beer in the other. "Aren't you gonna invite the kid in? Or do you plan to make him stand in the hundred-and-ten-degree heat until he passes out on your front stoop?"

Adam narrowed his eyes. "That's my dinner. Why don't you put it back where you found it before I have reason to make you?"

"Threatening the defenseless old man in charge of your career is hardly a wise move." Kyle headed for the living room to eat his prize, rather than the kitchen to put it away. "Let the kid in and close the damn door. My balls are sweating."

"Oh, for fuck's sake." Adam pinched his brow. "My career's over, anyway."

Which was true. Mostly. He had a fight coming up to defend his middleweight title. If he lost, that was it. Thirty-eight was near geriatric in the world of mixed martial arts, after all. Retirement was a logical next step. The only problem was, he had no clue what to do with his life if he quit fighting.

He rolled his shoulders. Now wasn't the time to worry about that. He'd worry when he lost, which he had no intention of doing. Not yet, at least. He turned his attention to his new personal assistant and gestured toward the bag at his feet. "Need help with that?"

"Ah, no, I've got it, but thanks." The man's voice broke midsentence, and if possible, his cheeks flared a deeper crimson. He ducked his chin, lifted his mammoth suitcase, and scurried over the threshold.

Adam suppressed a sigh and closed the door. He was used to people's fear. It was part of the package. Early in his career, following a brutal welterweight title fight where he'd KO'd the previous champ in the first thirty seconds of round one, he'd received a nickname—*the Beast*. Although it didn't suit his true personality, he'd bent to the expectations it demanded and adopted a public persona befitting the name.

Hoping to ease the man's apprehension, he offered a soft smile and stuck out his hand. "Since Kyle's too busy eating my dinner to introduce us, we'll have to handle the deed ourselves. Name's Adam. What's yours?"

The guy dropped his suitcase with a thud, winced, then took Adam's proffered hand with a small, clammy palm. "Beauregard Wilkins, Mr., ah, Mr. Beast, sir."

Stifling a laugh to conserve the poor man's dignity, Adam widened his grin instead. "Just Adam. No 'Beast' among friends and definitely no 'Mr.'" He folded his arms. The act reminded him of his shirtless, pantsless state. Perhaps the excessive blushing was less about dread and more about unease. Meeting your new boss in his underwear *would* be a tad uncomfortable, after all. "So, Beauregard, eh? Haven't heard that one in a while."

"Ah, actually, I prefer Bo." The tips of Bo's ears pinked. "If that's okay, sir."

Adam held up both hands. "Hey, it's your name, kid. I'll call you whatever you want me to call you, as long as you quit saying 'sir.' I may be at least two decades your senior, but I prefer not to be reminded of my old age within the comfort of my own home."

Bo swallowed, the bobbing lump at his throat belying his attempt at a calm, collected appearance. "It's not two decades, and I'm not a kid. I'm twenty-five." A hint of emotion, bordering on anger—or at the very least, frustration—flickered to life in his eyes. "I won't call you 'sir' if you don't call me 'kid.'"

The set of Bo's jaw and sureness of his words warred with the quiver in his voice. But damn if the contradiction of it all didn't send an unexpected zing of lust straight into Adam's groin. Especially with that hint of underlying courage and control despite his apparent nerves.

Nope. Not happening. Hooking up with an employee was never a good idea. Plus, Adam didn't do serious or long-term. He did short flings and one-night stands, neither of which would be advisable with someone he'd have to live with afterward. *Literally* live with. In the same house.

It didn't matter how adorable Bo was when he got grumpy or how much his lean frame and glasses totally did it for Adam. He was off-limits. A hard no.

Clearing his throat, Adam gave a curt nod and hid his smile. "Seems like a fair trade and a reasonable request." He nearly lost it when Bo arched a brow in response. The zing in his balls turned molten, and his dick twitched. Clothes needed to be bumped up the priority list. "Want me to show you where you'll be staying?"

"Yes, please."

Adam motioned toward the luggage at Bo's feet. "You sure I can't grab a bag?"

"No." Bo shook his head. He snatched up the suitcase, which was nearly the same size as him, and straightened his shoulders. "I've got it."

"Fair enough." Adam gestured Bo forward. "After you."

When Bo hobbled toward the stairs with his burdens, Adam coughed to hide a chuckle. Damn, this man was dangerous. He was adorkable in all the best ways. Pretty much Adam's catnip in walking, talking form.

A low groan slipped past Adam's lips when he mounted the stairs after Bo. Staring him straight in the face was one of the most delicious asses he'd ever seen. It was like someone had hand-picked Bo from a catalogue with all Adam's major weaknesses in mind.

Glasses. Slender but fit. Shy and awkward but with a spark of underlying fire. And that butt. Oh my God. Nothing quite got him like a nice round ass on an otherwise slim frame. The only thing missing was a passion for books.

Then again, if the beads of sweat breaking out on Bo's brow spoke anything to the weight of the suitcase he lugged behind him, there was a good chance it held more than clothes.

Deep, rumbling laughter sounded from the living room. Adam tore his attention from the eye-level temptation and narrowed his gaze.

Kyle winked and threw a finger gun Adam's direction when their eyes locked.

That bastard.

It appeared someone *had* hand-picked Bo for him. Someone who, despite being his manager of all things, couldn't grasp the concept behind Adam's refusal to date. Relationships only got in the way of success. He couldn't focus on his career—the very thing keeping food on both their plates—if he was gaga over some sexy little twink like Bo.

If his father had taught him nothing else, at least he'd instilled a sense of propriety.

"Everything okay?"

The note of concern in Bo's voice drew Adam's glare from Kyle. He softened his gaze before landing it on Bo. Any sign of the previous determined irritation had fled, replaced by pinched brows and a pout.

"Yeah, everything's fine." Adam smiled, willing his features neutral. "Your room is the second one on the left."

Bo nodded and returned to his slog, the suitcase banging against the uncarpeted wood as he tugged it up the stairs.

Before ascending out of view, Adam flipped Kyle the bird. He rolled his eyes when a cackle met the action.

He was so totally screwed.

Chapter Two

Bo dragged his suitcase into the room the Beast—no, make that *Adam*—had indicated as his. It was nearly the same size as the studio apartment he'd shared with his sister until only that very morning.

When he stopped short, a wall of barely clothed muscle bumped into his backside. He stumbled but didn't go sprawling the way his klutzy nature and forward momentum should've led him. Instead, a pair of strong, solid arms wrapped around his waist and hoisted him upright.

"Sorry about that. You okay?"

The gravelly voice washed over Bo, sending shivers in its wake. He licked his lips but made no move to leave the warm circle of Adam's unintentional embrace. "Ah, yep. Just dandy, thanks."

Ugh. What was his problem? Sure, he was shy, and awkward didn't even begin to cover the gamut of his quirks and mannerisms, but he wasn't usually *this* bad. He'd started plenty of new jobs where he'd squeaked by with only the minimal amount of additional nerve-related embarrassment. This was taking it to a whole new level of special.

Adam dropped his arms and stepped around Bo's frozen mortification. He picked up the oversized suitcase and tossed it onto the bed without the slightest hint of strain. As if the thing were full of feathers, not stocked to the gills with Bo's most precious possessions—his books.

"What'd you do, pack the kitchen sink in this thing?" Adam jutted his stubble-covered chin toward the bed as he scooped up Bo's duffel and tossed it next to the suitcase. "Didn't anyone tell you that's the first thing you leave behind?"

"It's, ah, actually filled with books."

Adam blinked a few times, then barked out a laugh. "Of course it is."

Bo ran his tongue over the back of his teeth, unsure what his new boss's reaction meant or how best to respond. He darted a nervous glance around the room, avoiding the temptation to linger over Adam's bare torso, and noted an empty bookshelf perfect for his treasures. He sucked in a breath. "Can I use that?"

Adam let loose a softer chuckle, motioning into the room with open arms. "This space is yours. Make yourself at home. You know, mi casa es su casa and all that jazz."

According to the research Bo had done before his interview, "the Beast" had quit high school the summer between sophomore and junior year to pursue his athletics. He also had a well-documented reputation for being the stereotypical dumb jock with a temper streak a mile long.

Bo's first impression of his new boss was therefore born of jealous frustration. If he'd been given the choice whether to drop out of high school or not, there was no question he would've stayed. But that luxury had disappeared when his father succumbed to his two-year battle with cancer. Only a few months into his eighteenth year and as many shy of graduation, Bo had taken over as sole caregiver of his eleven-year-old sister, Tallulah.

Little Lulu was now eighteen herself and heading off to chase her mechanical engineering dreams at the University of California, Berkeley. An expensive school made doubly so thanks to his insistence she stay in the dorms for her personal safety and to get the full college experience. Even with student loans, there was a hefty balance.

Bo had taken this job because it paid twice what he'd made laboring over eighty hours a week doing grunt work. It also offered a place to live as an added perk. Otherwise, he never would've worked for someone like Adam.

It wasn't that he had anything against professional athletes. More power to those individuals with the stamina and endurance to make a living with nothing more than their physical prowess and self-determination. But Adam "the Beast" Littrell was one of those guys who chewed up and spit out guys like Bo as a source of entertainment.

Which made their interactions thus far all the more perplexing. Aside from his near-nudity—and no apparent shame in that fact—Adam had been a complete gentleman.

Bo moved to the bed and unzipped his duffel bag, then extracted a fistful of boxer briefs. He cast a glance at Adam, who still hulked in the middle of the room like a sentinel. A very nearly naked sentinel. Bo swallowed. "If it's okay, I'm going to unpack."

Adam's gaze drifted to the underwear Bo clutched. He bit his lip, clearly struggling to suppress a grin.

Warmth crept up Bo's neck and heated his cheeks. He shoved the boxers out of sight between his duffel and suitcase. Was he destined to make a fool of himself at every turn?

"Yeah, yeah, no prob. I'll throw on some clothes and meet you downstairs." Adam brushed a thumb over his lips. Full, plump lips shadowed by salt-and-pepper stubble. The grin he'd failed at hiding lit his face with an unfair dose of beauty.

A man who'd taken countless blows to the head had no business being that handsome. Then again, a man like Bo had no business finding a man like Adam attractive in the first place. He was a celebrated athlete with all the world at his famously grumpy feet. Plus, he was Bo's boss.

Bo couldn't risk this opportunity. He might be only twenty-five, but he'd worked too hard to make ends meet the past seven years. No, even *thinking* about how sexy his new employer was would be out of the question. His focus needed to remain on the job and his baby sister. He might've missed all those once-in-a-lifetime experiences, but he'd do everything in his power to be sure Lulu wouldn't miss even one. Especially not because he'd been fired for lusting after his boss.

Landing this position with no previous experience in the field and a serious lack of formal education meant treading extra carefully to be sure his hotter-than-sin employer had no reason to reevaluate his decision.

"Take your time unpacking." Adam backed toward the door, rubbing a big meaty palm over his cropped brown hair. Threaded with silver, much like his facial hair, the distinguished air it gave Adam added to Bo's inappropriate longing. "When you're done, maybe we can grab something to eat and get to know each other. I'll even kick Kyle's dinner-stealing ass out so his ugly mug doesn't cause you to lose your appetite."

Bo snorted. Loud. With a complete lack of grace. He closed his eyes and wished himself invisible. "Yeah, okay, I'll be down in a jiffy."

A *jiffy?* What, was he eighty years old now? Where did these sayings keep coming from? Some secret store of humiliation tactics his brain kept stocked for such an occasion?

When Adam disappeared with a chuckle on his lips, Bo blew out a breath. He dropped his head back and cursed his idiocy before setting to work unpacking his meager possessions. He rarely spent frivolous money on himself. The books he owned were mostly from before his father died, aside from a limited few Lulu had insisted he purchase as Christmas and birthday presents from her.

By the time he'd emptied his duffel, the dresser was barely half full and a scant handful of shirts and pants graced the countless hangers in the large walk-in closet. He pulled the door closed, more embarrassed by his sparse wardrobe than he cared to admit.

He gave extra attention to unloading his books onto the gorgeous mahogany bookshelf that matched the luxurious bedroom set. His fingers traced over each well-worn cover as he nestled them together on the rich wood. Images of the tales hidden beneath danced through his mind.

When there was nothing left to unpack—and no more logical reasons to avoid the inevitable—Bo accepted his fate. He had to go downstairs. To have dinner with Adam. His new boss. *Not* someone he should be lusting after. Not even someone he should be considering friendship with.

Business only. Nothing more.

When Bo entered the living room, Adam was lounged on an overstuffed leather sofa watching football on a massive projector screen. The black T-shirt he now wore as a second skin over his sculpted torso rode up to display a deep, sexy V of muscle peeking out of a pair of basketball shorts—a physical feat Bo had never come close to achieving. His stomach was flat, but that had more to do with how little he ate than any purposeful attempt at maintaining his physique.

Adam leapt to his feet at a startling speed when Bo stepped into his line of sight. "Hey, I was beginning to think you'd smuggled yourself into Kyle's trunk, never to be seen again."

Bo drew back his chin. "Why would I sneak into Kyle's trunk?"

Adam shrugged and—was that a *blush*? His cheeks turned the loveliest shade of pink. He ducked his head, shoving his hands into the pockets of his baggy shorts. "You seemed a bit spooked. I thought you might be second-guessing your decision to work for someone with my reputation. I'm not known to be overly fun to be around, after all. Then, you know, I greeted you in my underwear. Not my finest hour."

A squeak escaped Bo's lips. He covered his mouth in horror, his eyes widening beneath the frames he'd knocked askew in the process.

He'd second-guessed his decision, all right. And the near-nudity *had* been a factor, but more due to fear of his own issues maintaining professionalism than any concern over Adam's lack thereof. Still, there was no turning back now. He'd already quit his other jobs. If he wanted to make Lulu's next tuition payment in full and on time, there was no escaping the decision he'd made. Whether it was his brightest move or not, he was stuck with Adam for a boss.

A big, sexy, blushing boss who had yet to live up to his well-known meathead status.

"Sorry about that, by the way. The no-clothes thing. I forgot you were coming. I'm a bit disorganized." Adam peered at Bo from his towering height, his lips tilted into a crooked, self-deprecating smirk. "Kinda why I need a PA. Someone's gotta look after my ass or I'll get myself into trouble."

Bo cleared his throat. Professional. He had to keep it professional. Even when his brain twisted Adam's words and produced an image of him getting paid to stare at his rock-hard backside.

Yeah. Especially then.

Squaring his shoulders, Bo forced a wide smile. "So,

boss, what's for dinner?"

Chapter Three

Adam flicked off the stove and moved the sauté pan to an unused burner to cool. He gave the red onions still sizzling at the bottom another cursory toss with the wooden spoon before angling a glance at Bo. His new PA leaned against the counter a few feet to his left, with a notepad and pencil in hand, observing and taking notes as Adam prepared their dinner.

Bo had offered to cook, as part of his job description included meal prep, but Adam insisted he take a night to settle in before jumping into his duties. Plus, with Adam's strict diet and the scarcity of food in the house, it would've been cruel to shove Bo into an unfamiliar kitchen and expect him to perform. Talk about starting off on the wrong foot.

Instead, Adam took the reins and suggested Bo make a grocery list for them while he scraped together a meal out of whatever he could find. As he cooked, Bo peppered him with questions about his diet. He scribbled notes as Adam told him about his favorite foods and recommended he check out the recipes his previous personal assistant had collected on a flash drive.

"Do you have any allergies I should know about? Or anything you don't particularly like?" Bo tapped the pencil against the corner of his glasses. His eyes never left Adam's hands as he mixed chopped raw spinach, the sautéed onions, fresh garlic, and an assortment of spices into half a pound of lean ground beef. "If not, I'm pretty creative in the kitchen. Maybe I can come up with a few new recipes that'll fit your diet requirements. Just for, you know, variety."

While Adam had gotten along well with Sasha, his previous PA, she'd never been one to go above and beyond the duties Adam asked of her. Hell, none of his PAs ever had. They stuck to the meal plan he provided and kept the refrigerator and cupboards stocked with the items he requested. There was no thinking outside the box. Already, Bo was proving to be a welcome change.

"No allergies, and I'm open to pretty much anything when it comes to food. As long as there's a lot of it, I'm game." Adam hid a grin as he formed the meat mixture into four similarly sized balls and placed them on a baking sheet. He slipped them into the preheated oven, set the timer for twelve minutes, and shifted his focus to the boiling water. "Could you grab the pasta?"

Bo snapped to attention, plucking the spinach noodles off the counter with such gusto they nearly went flying out of his hand. He fumbled the package a few times before handing it to Adam without making eye contact. He licked his lips and returned his rapt gaze to the pad in front of him, as if it held the answers to the universe's most intriguing questions.

"Thanks, my man." Adam chuckled under his breath and left Bo in peace to work through his awkward moment. Sure, he might be a little nervous, but his reactions didn't fit the usual fear response Adam received from the public. It was refreshing as hell and deserved all the silent encouragement Adam could offer.

He let the pasta boil for six minutes, drained the noodles over the sink, then stirred in a handful of cherry tomatoes, spinach, and low-fat parmesan cheese. When the timer went off for the meatballs, he pulled them out of the oven and tonged them into the pasta bowl.

"Ta-da." Adam cracked a grin and waved a theatrical arm toward his finished product. "Mr. Wilkins, I'd like you to meet my lean beef spinach meatball pasta. Hope you're hungry."

Bo's nostrils flared as he sniffed the air and returned Adam's grin with a shy smile. "Smells delicious."

They doled out two helpings—Adam's significantly larger than Bo's—and sat down at the breakfast bar. Although he rarely drank, Adam offered to pop a bottle of wine with the meal and was pleased when Bo accepted.

Conversation was sparse at first, but as the alcohol worked its magic, Bo loosened up enough to answer a few of Adam's casual questions. He even asked a few of his own. By the time they parted ways for the evening, after teaming up to put away the leftovers and do the dishes, Adam was thoroughly convinced Kyle had to die.

What had possessed him to bring a man like Bo into Adam's life? Now, of all times? The pressure to focus and succeed was at its highest in ages, and his goddamn manager decided to introduce a distraction of epic proportions.

Yeah, Kyle needed his head pounded. Or at the very least, he was going to get one hell of an earful.

For Bo's first official day on the job, Adam drove himself to the gym, as he'd been doing for the past few weeks. Eventually, he'd have Bo take him, but for now he left his new PA to familiarize himself with the house. After all, he had the ultimate challenge of tackling the disaster Adam had created since Sasha's departure.

It wasn't that Adam was a slob per se, but cleaning, laundry, and overall organizational skills weren't his strong points. When left to his own devices, things tended to get out of hand. Fast.

The smell of fresh laundry mixed with strong cleaning chemicals assaulted Adam's senses the moment he walked through the garage door after his morning training. He scrunched his nose in protest. The clean linen smell was pleasant, but what the hell kind of biochemical warfare was Bo waging on his home? The pungent scent of corrosive bleach and all manner of other caustic solutions burned his nostrils and left his head spinning.

He headed for the laundry room to drop off his gym bag and found Bo on his hands and knees in the hallway, scrubbing at the stone tile flooring.

"Fuckin' hell, Bo, you're gonna asphyxiate from all these fumes." Adam tossed his bag down the hall in the general direction of the laundry room. "Why don't you take a break? We can grab lunch somewhere and hit the grocery while we're out."

Bo sat back on his haunches and swiped a wrist over his brow. "I'm almost done here any—" His eyes bugged, and he scurried to his feet, the sponge dropping from his hand. "Holy crap on a cracker, what the heck happened to you?"

Adam froze when Bo's soapy fingertips grazed his jaw. A jolt of electricity fired under his skin at the connection. He followed the tingling path of Bo's touch with his own fingers, marveling at the intensity of the impression that brief contact left behind.

"Did you get jumped?" Bo's brows pinched, his lips turning down at the corners. "Did you call the police? Are you hurt anywhere else?"

A laugh bubbled up Adam's throat at the unexpected

barrage of questions and the look of genuine concern twisting Bo's face. When was the last time anyone cared he'd been hurt? Hell, unless they bordered on life-threatening, even he failed to notice his injuries more often than not. So was the life of a mixed martial arts fighter. Sparring was the best way to train, and sparring equaled wounds. Rarely as intense as those suffered at an official fight, but colorful and bloody nonetheless.

"I'm fine. Just a few scratches." Adam tried to grin, but the act tugged at his already split lip and fresh blood trickled down his chin.

Bo gasped and clamped a hand over Adam's wrist. "That's more than a scratch. Where's your first aid kit?"

"First aid kit?" Adam cocked a brow. He didn't keep anything like that at home. If his injuries required mending, Eddie, his coach, would tend to him after he hit the showers. Today, the damage was minimal, so he'd left without patching up.

Gaping, Bo shook his head. "Don't tell me you get beat up for a living and don't keep basic first aid supplies around the house."

Adam knuckled the blood off his chin and shrugged. "It's a split lip. I'll be fine."

"A split lip, a black eye, and a gashed eyebrow. That is not fine." Bo scowled and dropped Adam's wrist with an adorable little huff. "I'm adding medical supplies to the grocery list. If you're going to come home looking like roadkill on a regular basis, I'm going to need some necessities. In the meantime, will you at least let me put some ice on that eye?"

Biting back a grin that would worsen the bleeding and increase Bo's worry, Adam allowed Bo to latch on to his wrist a second time and tug him toward the kitchen. He reveled in the soft warmth of Bo's touch and the gentle care behind his fussing.

No one had ever clucked and cooed over Adam's

wounds the way Bo did now, least of all one of his personal assistants. Even his own mother had always taken a standoffish approach, far preferring to fret over her latest high-dollar antique purchase than anything transpiring in the life of her only child. Her lack of a mothering nature had gone a long way toward building up the tough exterior he relied on today, but it had also destroyed any chance of a future relationship between them.

After his father pulled him out of high school to focus full-time on prepping for his debut in the octagon, Adam had barely seen his mother. The last time was over five years prior, purely by happenstance when he ran into her at the airport, of all places. They'd exchanged cordial pleasantries and escaped to their respective terminals without sparing the other a backward glance.

Now, as a near-stranger held a homemade ice pack to his throbbing brow and offered a cool washcloth for him to press over his swollen lip, Adam's heart skittered to a brief halt before doing a somersault and kicking back to life. He'd never been pampered before, but it was something he could get used to.

Chapter Four

Bo clutched two steaming cups of coffee as he stood outside Adam's bedroom door. It was barely a quarter past six in the morning. Not early in his world, considering he used to wake up at 4:00 a.m. every day, but Adam had proven to be every bit of the challenge Kyle had promised he'd be, no matter the time.

When Bo first interviewed to be Adam's personal assistant, one of Kyle's questions had hedged around whether he would be comfortable "getting physical." When he'd asked what that meant, Kyle had smirked and replied, "Adam Littrell is the furthest thing from a morning person you'll ever meet. As his PA, it'll be your job to get his ass outta bed. That takes several high-octane doses of coffee and a whole helluva lot of elbow grease."

This was the third morning in a row Bo had faced down Adam's door with high-test caffeine in hand, and the third morning in a row his stomach had tied itself into knots.

That first day had been the worst. Building up the

courage to waltz into his boss's room while he still slept, although blatantly invited and entirely expected, had taken every ounce of reserves Bo had left.

He'd almost turned tail and run when he found Adam tangled in his sheets and wearing nothing but a pair of form-fitting boxer briefs. Especially when realization dawned that his next move required crawling onto the massive bed and laying his hands on Adam's bare sleep-warm skin. Somehow, he'd managed it, and after what had proven to be more of a workout than even Kyle had predicted, Adam eventually stirred.

Despite having two successful victories under his belt, nerves still wound their way through Bo's belly at the thought of barreling into Adam's room and shaking him awake. It was his job. Adam relied on him to help get his day started. That was all it was. It was as innocent as a parent waking a child for school. It had nothing to do with the heated fantasies that kept Bo up into the wee hours of the night.

Everything between them was platonic and professional. Nothing more. He needed to keep that at the forefront of his mind or these wakeups might end him.

Clearing his throat, Bo dialed up his courage, shifted the mug handles into one hand, and pushed through the door. As with the previous two mornings, a faint light from the bathroom spilled into the room and caught on Adam's slumbering form. If the twisted disaster of his blankets had anything to say about it, Adam was a fitful sleeper—something that seemed at odds with the near-impossibility of rousing him in the mornings. But seriously, it looked like he shared the bed with a cyclone.

Bo stepped into the room and set both coffees on Adam's nightstand. He curled his lips between his teeth when Adam snuffled, rolled over, and splayed out one perfectly sculpted arm, almost as if he were reaching out to Bo in his sleep. The thought sent Bo's already ravaged stomach churning anew. He blew out a steadying breath before easing onto the bed, biting his tongue, and giving Adam a pointed shove.

With a soft smacking of his lips, Adam turned his head away but showed no other sign he'd registered Bo's presence. Inching a little closer, Bo angled his knees for leverage and laid both hands on the firm warmth of Adam's shoulder. This time he shook with all his might, calling Adam's name as he did.

A startled snort signaled Adam's first step into the land of the living. Bo let go as soon as those sleep-heavy gray eyes fluttered open and locked on to his own. He leaned over, grabbed the first cup of coffee, and held it out as the peace offering it was. "Morning. Sorry. Hope I didn't scare you."

Adam slow-blinked a few times before scrubbing a hand over his face and pushing to an elbow. The muscles in his chest and shoulders rippled beneath his taut skin, their contours sharpened by the shadows thrown from the dim bathroom light. He accepted the caffeinated liquid and grunted in thanks before downing the whole thing in one long swallow.

After taking the empty mug from Adam, Bo hopped off the bed. He gripped the porcelain between both palms and stared into the dregs Adam left behind to keep his eyes from wandering over his boss's naked torso as he stretched himself awake.

"Thanks for the go-go juice, my man." Adam yawned, and his jaw cracked with the movement. He fluffed up his pillow and leaned against the headboard. "What's on the agenda today? Anything mind-numbingly boring I should start planning an out for now?"

Bo snapped his gaze to Adam's, swallowing a whimper at the sight of his sleep-mussed hair and lazy morning smile. He set the empty cup on the nightstand, scooped up the full one, and passed it to Adam. He'd already learned one cup was never enough, and discussing the monotonous details of Adam's schedule always went over better paired with that extra jolt of caffeine. "Other than your regular training, Eddie is supposed to come by this afternoon with some more footage of Zaragoza for you to review. Oh, and Kyle wanted to go over a few new proposals for sponsorship contracts. He said he'd be around before dinner."

"Of course he did." Adam huffed out a laugh, then brought the mug to his lips. The second cup always went down with a little less desperation than the first. More sipping, less gulping. "The damn parasite just wants a free meal."

Offering a noncommittal hum in response, Bo backed toward the door. He needed to break free before Adam tossed off the covers and gave him any more fodder for his relentless imagination. "I'll get your shake started. Are you feeling chocolate or vanilla this morning?"

"Mmm, chocolate." Adam purred the response, and Bo had to suppress a moan at the inappropriate thoughts that throaty morning voice inspired. He mumbled a response and hurried from the room before Adam had a chance to say anything else or reveal more skin.

When Adam shuffled into the kitchen fifteen minutes later clad in his standard workout attire, a duffel bag filled with clean clothes tossed over his shoulder, Bo curled his toes into the tile to ground himself. He'd gotten up a little early that morning to surprise Adam with one of the new recipes he'd hunted down on the internet, but now the jitters were getting the better of him. What if Adam hated what he'd made? What if he skipped breakfast on purpose or felt obligated to eat Bo's offering, then wound up with acid reflux or sluggish reflexes as a result?

Adam tilted his chin and sniffed the air. "Smells more chocolaty than normal. I like it. What is that?"

Swallowing past the nerves constricting his throat, Bo pointed to a Tupperware container sitting beside the blender bottle with Adam's post-workout coconut milk and chocolate whey protein shake. "I, ah, made you some vegan fudge fat bombs. I know how much you love chocolate, and the website I found the recipe on said fat bombs are good preworkout snacks. Don't feel like you have to—"

"You made me fat bombs?" Adam's face lit up like a child who'd spotted a pile of birthday presents. After dropping his bag, he lunged for the Tupperware, tore off the lid, and grinned at the lumpy brown balls inside. "*Chocolate* fat bombs?"

Before Bo could think of a sensible response, Adam lifted one of the treats to his mouth. He closed his eyes as he took a bite, letting his head fall back on a decadent, throaty little moan. "Oh my God, dude, I could kiss you right now."

Bo squirmed under the intoxicating effect of those words. It was a simple turn of phrase, not one Adam truly meant, but it made the hairs at Bo's nape stand at attention and a shiver run down his spine.

He had to get himself in check. Lusting after his boss was the last thing he needed right now. With a false bravado born only from the desperation to do something—anything—to distract his errant thoughts, Bo palmed Adam's keys. He'd managed to score a brief reprieve from the driving duties that came with his position by keeping busy around the house the first few days, but he couldn't avoid it forever. Part of his job included chauffeuring Adam through the city, after all.

Thus far, Adam wasn't aware of Bo's moderate—okay, more like moderately huge—fear of driving. Even in his small hometown of Indian Springs, Nevada, with only a few hundred permanent residents and no hope of tourist traffic, Bo had been on edge navigating the roads. The thought of facing the busy Las Vegas streets downright terrified him.

But he was doing this for Lulu. He could handle a few measly hours of driving every week if it meant his little sister could go to the school of her dreams and have extra spending cash to enjoy life to the fullest while she was there.

"How about a ride to the gym?" Bo forced a smile. "You can eat while I drive."

Adam stopped midchew and cocked a questioning brow. "Are you sure?"

A slightly delirious laugh bubbled up Bo's throat. He straightened his shoulders and nodded. "Why wouldn't I be?"

"I kinda got the impression driving wasn't your cuppa tea." Adam snapped the lid closed on the Tupperware and scooped up his duffel bag. He slipped both the fat bombs and his protein shake into the front mesh pocket. "It isn't a requirement. I can drive myself."

Okay, so maybe Adam *was* aware of his ridiculous fear. All the more reason to overcome it. "No, no, I'm good. I was trying to get my head wrapped around the job the past few days, but I'm ready to hit the ground running now."

Adam ran his tongue in a slow, mesmerizing circle, wetting every inch of his lips before smacking them together and offering a nod. "All righty then. Let's bounce."

As they headed toward the garage, the warm weight of Adam's hand landed on Bo's shoulder. When Bo angled a glance his way, Adam gave a toothy grin. "Thank you. For everything. I'm not really used to people paying attention the way you do. It's nice."

Heat spread up Bo's neck to bite at his cheeks. He ducked his head. "It's no big deal."

"Yeah, well, I think it is." Adam gave Bo's shoulder a gentle squeeze before moving his hand away. He opened the door to the garage and gestured Bo forward. "Let's hit the streets, shall we?"

Chapter Five

"Why do you seem grumpier than usual?" Kyle pounded a fist into Adam's shoulder before shielding his eyes against the late-afternoon sun. "By now, I thought you'd be singing off-key renditions of those corny-ass musicals you love so much and driving me up a goddamn wall."

"Shut the fuck up." Adam dumped his gym bag onto the pavement and glowered at his manager. "Your little plan has fully and totally backfired, dickhead."

"Oh?" Humor laced Kyle's voice as he dropped his hand and squinted instead. "What's wrong? I thought Bo was just your style."

Adam cracked his knuckles and averted his gaze. He couldn't let on how true that statement was or Kyle would never let him live it down. "For a quick fuck, sure. But you went and moved the guy in with me. He does my laundry, for Christ's sake. And scrapes my ass outta bed in the mornings. Not an ideal situation for fun in the bedroom. Might make things kinda awkward after."

Kyle had the nerve to laugh. No, not laugh, but full-on guffaw. The sun flashed off his pearly whites, the brightness a sharp contrast to the smooth mahogany of his skin. Even at nearly twenty-five years Adam's senior, Kyle could pass for ten years his junior. Especially with his short braided dreads that had barely a trace of gray. The exact opposite of Adam's silver-streaked crop of hair.

He really was getting old. Too old, if his screaming body had anything to say about it. His workout had been intense, but no more so than his dailies ever were. Yet his muscles ached and his energy had waned so much by the end, he'd tapped out of a scrimmage he should've easily won.

"Did you ever think of trying something other than a 'quick fuck'?" Kyle sucked his teeth and shook his head. "I was hoping you might find a slice of happiness to call your own outside the ol' bump and grind. You deserve a little companionship beyond these old bones and the random bodies you pound to a pulp then forget. Both in and out of the ring."

Adam had no interest in the kind of relationship Kyle was insinuating he needed. While his career was still viable, he couldn't afford the distraction. Even if Bo proved to be quite a delectable distraction indeed.

Kyle landed another blow to Adam's shoulder. As a retired brawler, his hits still packed a mean punch. Adam covered his wince with a snarl. "Watch it, Grandpa. I didn't sleep well last night. I'm tired and cranky."

"You're full of excuses today, aren't you?" Kyle rolled his eyes. "You're thirty-eight, my man. It's time to think about settling down. Starting a family. Maybe make some little Beasts I can bounce on my knee and tell stories to about their pop's golden years."

It was Adam's turn to send his gaze to the heavens as his silver Mercedes-Maybach pulled up to the curb with Bo at the helm. Right on time. The trunk popped, and Adam rounded the sleek sedan to stash his bag. He shot a quick wink at Kyle from beneath its protective shield. Although he'd meant most of what he said—living with Bo had proven to be more challenging than he'd ever imagined—he didn't want the old man to think he was truly angry with him.

Being the Beast meant playing a part when he was in the public eye. True, he'd taken that role a bit further than usual today, but he really was exhausted. And his advancing age was only part of the problem.

He hadn't lied about sleeping poorly. He'd tossed and turned the previous night, and the six before.

Beauregard Wilkins's irresistible little ass was to blame there. Knowing he was asleep a few doors down did unspeakable things to Adam's libido. Unspeakable things that were 100 percent not allowed, which meant he wanted them even more.

He'd never been one to back down from a challenge, and that's what Bo represented. Fighting the urge to claim his kissable lips had Adam distracted when he should be focused on training.

The sexual tension sizzling between them couldn't be denied, yet Bo made sure to keep their professional relationship at the forefront of every interaction. There was never any doubt where he stood, even when Adam caught his gaze drifting somewhere decidedly nonwork-related.

Somewhere that twitched in Adam's pants at the mere thought of Bo's gorgeous green eyes widening behind his glasses when he realized he'd been caught. On more than one occasion.

Fending back a grin, Adam closed the trunk, clapped Kyle on the shoulder, then slipped into the cool interior of his favorite ride. His stomach took a dip when his gaze met Bo's wild eyes, his hands clutching the steering wheel at ten and two like the good little terrified Vegas driver he was.

"Bo?" Adam furrowed his brow. The dude looked seriously rattled. "You want me to drive home?"

Adam's gym was located off the Strip, but not by much. It was in Paradise, off Tropicana, which meant the most efficient way to get from his home in Enterprise was straight over Las Vegas Boulevard. Every time Bo made the trip, he turned a little greener around the gills.

This time, he looked damn near death. He was pallid and sickly, a sheen of sweat beaded on his brow.

"No, nope, I'm fine." A shaky smile tugged at Bo's lips, then fell into a pout. "I can do this. I promise. I'm fine. I'll be fine."

Adam angled toward Bo and cocked his head. "I don't doubt that, but I also don't mind driving. In fact, I love it. It's easier to hitch a ride because parking can be a challenge, but I'd be more than happy to drive myself—"

"No." Bo's knuckles turned white as he gripped the steering wheel with more force, his face pinching. "This is part of my job. I can do it. I'm fine."

Driving in Vegas wasn't for the faint of heart, especially not around the Strip. Adam couldn't blame Bo for being a wreck, especially since he came from a small town well outside the city limits. He'd admitted to only visiting the touristy areas a handful of times in his life, and most of those had been before he was old enough to enjoy what it had to offer.

That was something Adam intended to change. He might have to keep his hands—and his other body parts—to himself, but that didn't mean he couldn't enjoy Bo's company in other, more platonic ways. It wasn't the relationship Kyle had wanted him to find, but he could meet him halfway. A friendship was safe. It wouldn't distract him too much or risk taking his head out of the game.

"Hey, I'm not doubting your abilities. I wouldn't mind, especially not for my workouts. There's usually parking around back. I'm being lazy by having you drive me, if we're being honest." He wasn't sure why, but something told him to tack on another reassurance. "Your job isn't in jeopardy. I trust you'd be here if I needed you, but I'm okay to drive myself."

Bo deflated, his forehead banging against the steering wheel as his shoulders sagged forward. "Why are you so nice to me all the time? I thought you were supposed to be a dick."

When Bo's head whipped up in alarm at his own words, a full belly laugh replaced the snicker that nearly escaped Adam's lips.

"I-I didn't mean that. I'm sorry. You're my boss. You're not a... a *dick*."

Adam swiped his hand through the air to dismiss Bo's apology. "No worries. I'm used to it. I've gotta give off that dick vibe or my opponents won't be intimidated. If they knew who I really was, they'd laugh me outta the octagon."

Bo pressed his lips together. "And who are you, really?"

A thought sparked to life, and Adam rubbed his palms together. It was time to give Bo a better idea of just who he worked for.

Glancing at his phone, Adam grinned. It was still early—especially by Vegas standards—and it was Saturday night. Sundays were the only day he took off, unless he was in a training camp, so the timing couldn't be more perfect.

He tapped the unlock code, then swiped the phone open. Bo frowned at him, but Adam focused his attention on the task at hand. Once done, he set his cell in the cup holder and pointed at Bo's seat belt. "Off with that thing and switch seats with me. I'm driving."

"No, I told you, I can—"

"This has nothing to do with any perceived inability on your end. I *want* to drive." Adam pressed the button to release Bo's belt. "Plus, where we're going is a surprise."

Bo's face scrunched into an adorable, confused mess. His lip curled, his nose wrinkled, and his brows pinched.

"A surprise?"

"Yes, a surprise. Now out." Adam opened his door, exited the car, and hurried to the driver's side, where Bo had yet to move a muscle. He gave the door a jerk, then wrapped a hand around Bo's slender arm. "Come on. Unless you have something else planned for this evening.... Shit. I didn't even think to ask. Do you?"

"Do I what?"

Adam chuckled. "Do you have plans? It's Saturday night. That was presumptuous of me to assume you didn't."

Bo was beautiful, after all. He probably had a hot date. Or hell, for all Adam knew, he intended to spend the night with his significant other. That wasn't out of the realm of possibilities. Their casual conversation over the past week had steered mostly clear of personal details.

A ridiculous pang of what could only be jealousy lanced through Adam's gut. Since when did he get jealous? Since never, that's when. He scowled.

Bo swallowed and slid out of the car. "I was planning to do a couple loads of laundry."

Maybe that was it. Maybe it was the domesticity. Adam's previous personal assistants had either been female or straight. There hadn't been a lick of attraction between them. But this was different. Bo was different. When he washed Adam's clothes, prattled on about his schedule for the day, or roused him out of bed with a cup of coffee and a precious little shove, it didn't feel the way it had with the others. It felt almost intimate.

Adam pointed toward the passenger seat. "Laundry can wait. Hop in."

Bo obliged without argument, but as they buckled up and Adam shifted into Drive, he cleared his throat. "Where are we going, exactly?"

Tossing Bo a wink, Adam eased into traffic. "I'm gonna show you the man behind the Beast."

Chapter Six

66 I still don't get why we couldn't stop at the house for a change of clothes. It isn't that far." Bo fidgeted in his new pair of distressed leather Ariat boots. He tugged on the cuffs of the slate-gray button-down Adam had picked out for him and tried not to think about how much it had all cost. The designer jeans alone had been over two hundred dollars. "This seems excessive."

Adam tucked his wallet into the back pocket of his own newly purchased dark-washed jeans. He thanked the cashier and accepted the shopping bags that held the casual clothes they'd worn into the store. He turned from the counter and met Bo's wary gaze. "Because, young grasshopper, shopping is part of the experience. I said I'd show you the real me, and this is part of the package. I'm a total diva when it comes to clothes. Only the best."

He brushed an invisible spec of lint from the front of his shirt and flashed a grin so toothy and wide, Bo couldn't help but return it with one of his own. "Plus, it's no fun if you don't have some swagger for your first night under the Vegas lights. And you will, Mr. Wilkins, because you're lookin' good." Adam jogged his brows and motioned toward the exit. "Ready to get this party started?"

The fabric of Adam's black-and-white pinstriped dress shirt hugged his broad shoulders, the muscles beneath rippling as he guided Bo out the door. It was a distraction, but Bo forced his eyes to meet Adam's twinkling gray irises rather than roam where they didn't belong. At least Adam was fully dressed. Although, that didn't help much, considering the sinful way clothes clung to his body.

Licking his lips, Bo shifted his gaze to the busy crawl of humans choking the sidewalk around them. "You clean up pretty well yourself."

Adam laughed, the deep vibrato humming through Bo with the same familiar comfort of music played too loud in the car. What would it feel like to press against him when he made that sound? Would it cause Bo's skin to prickle and the nerves to dance beneath his skin?

Bo squared his shoulders. He had to stop thinking like that. Adam was off-limits. Lusting after his boss wasn't only stupid, it was also making his daily grind a challenge.

It wasn't the first time he'd ever found someone attractive, but it *was* the first time he'd had to crawl into bed with said someone every morning. Bo shivered at the thought of touching Adam's bare skin, sleep-warm and rock-solid. He groaned and shook his head. He had to focus.

Steering his attention back to the present, Bo held out a hand. "I can take the bags."

Instead of passing them over, Adam slung the shopping bags over his shoulder, supporting them with a casual crooked finger. The result was something straight out of a fashion magazine. Especially when he cocked his head and offered a model-perfect grin.

"We've got plenty of time. Why don't we drop them off at the car and grab some dinner first?"

Bo bit his lip. He'd fought Adam on the clothes, but the man had insisted he consider them a work uniform. Just one of the perks of the job. It was an excuse, but Bo had caved anyway. He didn't own anything half this nice. He'd save them for work-related events. Turn the excuse into a truth.

But now dinner? And what did Adam have planned for after? Bo made a mental list of his available funds and came up short. Very short. Still, that didn't mean he'd let Adam pay. This evening—whatever it was—had nothing to do with work.

"I'm really not hungry, but if you—" A boisterous group crowded out of the nearest casino entrance, their squeals and high-pitched cackles drawing Bo's attention. At least a dozen women, all wearing or carrying various accoutrements shaped like penises, shoved past them. Bo stumbled and collided with Adam, who dropped their bags to steady him against his chest.

For the second time in less than a week Bo found himself encircled in Adam's warm, solid embrace. And for the second time he made zero efforts to leave it.

Adam chuckled. Although it wasn't a full-on laugh, Bo's earlier suspicions were confirmed. His skin tingled and every nerve in his body thrummed as Adam's chest rumbled against his.

"Gotta watch out for those bachelorette parties. They're liable to stampede you flat."

Bo nodded, relishing the soft cotton against his cheek. He longed to rest his head on Adam's chest, wrap his arms around him, and drift on a rush of euphoric endorphins.

But he shouldn't. No, he *couldn't*.

He took a deliberate step back. Adam's arms tightened briefly before falling away, as if creating the distance had been as hard on him as it had been on Bo.

Bending to scoop up their bags, Adam jerked his chin down the Strip in the direction the horde of raucous, penis-wielding women had gone. "Come on. Hungry or not, I guarantee you'll make room for Giada."

"Giada?" Bo pinched his brow. That sounded expensive.

Adam tossed their bags over his shoulder in that GQ-chic way that conflicted so acutely with his Beast persona. He rubbed his other hand over the scruff on his chin. "Giada De Laurentiis is a brilliant celebrity chef. She also happens to be a big fan of UFC. We've become friends over the years. I'll hook her up with tickets now and again, and she returns the favor by making sure there's always a table at Giada for me. Your mouth will thank me later, I promise."

A zing shot straight into Bo's balls when he thought of all the ways he could thank Adam with his mouth. He ran a shaking hand through his hair. "That sounds great, but I'm really not hun—"

A warm, callused palm met Bo's. His stomach jerked in tandem with the tug Adam gave on his hand.

"Just take one bite and I swear you'll be singing a different tune." Adam pulled Bo into the throng of humans, his grip tightening when the jostle of the moving crowd had Bo tripping over his own feet. "Tonight's on me. Go hog-wild. Buy one of everything on the menu, if you want. You won't regret a single morsel that hits your tongue."

Bo groaned, thankful the commotion around them covered the noise. His dick tingled to life as more images of his tongue on Adam's many tasty "morsels" flooded his brain.

Adam charged ahead, his firm grasp a welcome comfort as the bustling mob pressed in from all sides. Bo hurried to keep pace, his roaming thoughts spurred on by the view of Adam's perfect backside.

By the time they'd dumped their bags at the car and Adam had schmoozed their way into the restaurant, Bo's racing heart had more to do with his dirty mind than their clipped pace.

Preferring not to make a scene, he acquiesced—again—and enjoyed one of the best meals of his life. Just as Adam had promised. Still, Adam's moans and whimpers as he relished his food, paired with the many times he licked his lips and the way he placed each bite deliberately into his mouth, had Bo shifting in his seat.

As they devoured their meals, they talked about everything and nothing. The careful guard Bo kept in place slipped, and he found himself not only laughing at Adam's stories, but telling some of his own.

His heart fluttered when Adam took his hand again to lead him through the thickening crowd. As if it meant nothing. As if that single act didn't throw Bo's entire system out of whack.

"Where are we going?" Bo struggled to keep up as Adam's intimidating bulk parted the sea of humans and his long legs strode purposefully ahead.

Adam tossed a wink and a cheeky grin over his shoulder. "I told you, it's a surprise."

Over the past week, Bo had caught glimpses of the lighthearted, fun-loving man currently tugging him down the congested Strip. Although at apparent odds with the reputation Bo had read about, this side of Adam felt increasingly genuine. Like the jerky meathead he was so well known to be was the real act, and this soft, sweet, goofy side was his true persona.

Bo was in so much trouble. The more time he spent with this kind, charming, and decidedly non-Beast of a man, the more that physical pull became something much stronger. Lusting was bad enough. He couldn't start crushing on his boss. No way, nohow.

But when Adam led him into the Planet Hollywood hotel and dragged him to the Will Call box office outside the V Theater, every bit of his self-determination went soaring out the window.

Bo flashed back to Adam's twinkling eyes as he'd

winked and said, *I'm gonna show you the man behind the Beast.* This was it. This was the defining moment. The big "reveal" of Adam's true self. And it came in the form of *Evil Dead The Musical.*

Why that twisted Bo's heart and brought a grin to his lips, he might never understand. But it did. *Ho boy,* did it ever.

Adam dropped Bo's hand to fork over his ID and a credit card and received two tickets in return. He waved them in the air, his face beaming with joy. "I hope you aren't too attached to those clothes."

"Uh...." Bo glanced at his brand-new outfit. He screwed up his face. "Actually, I've grown quite fond of them."

Adam accepted two white T-shirts from the woman behind the ticket window. He handed one to Bo, then shook out the other and held it out for Bo to see. In bloodred letters, it screamed, *"Evil Dead The Musical.* I survived The Splatter Zone."

Shaking his head, Bo took a step back. "Nuh-uh. No way."

"Yes huh, and yes way." Adam grinned and pulled the shirt over his head. "Go on, garb up. This is a once-in-a-lifetime experience you'll never forget. I promise."

"But—"

"No buts." Adam snatched Bo's shirt out of his hands. "Arms up. You either work with me here or I'll resort to tickling."

Bo instinctively pressed his arms closer to his sides to protect his most vulnerable ticklish spots. "You wouldn't dare."

"I would, and I have. Ask Kyle's cranky ass. I had to fight him on this too. He didn't regret it, and neither will you."

With a sigh, Bo raised his arms. The oversized shirt would do very little to protect his beautiful new clothes, but the look of childish delight on Adam's face was all the convincing he needed.

Whatever lay ahead, it would be worth it to see Adam this happy.

As Adam latched on to his hand and marched toward the theater entrance with an unstoppable grin spreading his cheeks, Bo accepted defeat. How in Hades was he supposed to *not* crush on a man that perfect?

They took their seats—front and center, no less—and Adam pumped a fist into the air. One of the crew members scurrying around the stage gave him a thumbs-up in response.

"Once in a lifetime, huh?" Bo rolled his eyes.

Adam offered an innocent shrug, followed by a wicked grin. "Once-in-a-lifetime experiences can be repeated, ya know. Plus, half the fun is singing along. How're you supposed to do that if you haven't seen it before to learn the words?"

Yep. He was in serious trouble. The man behind the Beast had his claws in Bo's heart, whether he wanted him to or not.

Chapter Seven

The heavenly aroma of fresh-brewed coffee tugged at Adam's senses, but he fought the urge to wake. His current dream was far too enjoyable to give in to consciousness. Within the constructs of his fantasy world, Bo nestled in his arms. The solid warmth of his body tucked into Adam's, and soft snoring met Adam's ear.

He entangled their legs further, marveling at how their bodies fit together like puzzle pieces. The silky waves of Bo's hair tickled Adam's chin as he nuzzled into Adam's neck and snuggled closer.

It was perfect. The epitome of what a dreamworld should be. He ran a lazy hand up and down Bo's back, relishing the murmuring hum and the languid little hip roll that followed.

When the quiet snores returned and Bo stilled in his arms once more, Adam's lids drifted open. He blinked against the brightness. Once, twice, a third time.

What the hell?

Lucidity replaced the hazy fragments of sleep. He wasn't in his bedroom, nor was he alone.

As surely as he'd been in Adam's dream, Bo pressed into Adam's chest. His lanky limbs wrapped around Adam like a vine, and the soft, woodsy scent of his shampoo warred with the heady smell of coffee.

How had they wound up squashed onto the couch together? Adam did a quick mental check, running through the events of the previous evening. After they'd returned home from the show, they'd gone their separate ways to shower off the sticky fake blood. Bo had demanded Adam return with his clothes so he could attempt to rid them of the vivid red stains.

While Bo scrubbed and pretreated the ever-loving hell out of the garments, Adam had made air-popped popcorn. Then they'd settled on the couch and watched another of his favorite cult classic musicals—*The Rocky Horror Picture Show*.

And then.... *Right*. After Bo had tended to the laundry—switching some to the dryer and laying the rest out to air-dry—he'd landed face-first on the couch and almost immediately fallen asleep.

Not quite ready for sleep himself, Adam had put in *Shock Treatment*, the follow-up to *Rocky Horror*, and proceeded to pass out sitting up not long after. At some point during the night, Bo had crawled halfway into Adam's lap. Too exhausted to drag his lazy ass to bed—and, quite frankly, enjoying the closeness to Bo—Adam had shifted them into the position they were in now.

Well, he'd parked Bo in front of him so they could both stretch out, but the vine-like attachment had been all Bo. Not that Adam minded. At all.

Shit. Sleeping with your employee—even fully clothed and with no naughty business—was a big no-no. It crossed damn near every boundary possible.

So why wasn't he leaping off the couch and fleeing

the scene?

Bo jerked in his sleep, snorted in alarm, then clung even tighter. He burrowed his face into Adam's chest, and any thought of running disappeared without a trace.

Instead, Adam resumed the gentle caress of Bo's back, who rewarded him with the same sleepy humming noises and another hip roll. Only this time, something hard pressed into Adam's hip bone and a low moan replaced the soft murmurs.

Double shit.

Propriety overruled Adam's desire to join Bo in the grind and groan. But barely.

"Bo?" When he didn't stir, Adam cleared his throat to loosen the morning gravel of his voice and tried again. "Bo?"

Rather than startling awake and bolting in horror as Adam had so feared, Bo made adorable lip-smacking noises and snuggled in closer. "Mmm. Mornin'."

"Ah, good morning."

"Need. Coffee." Bo's jaw cracked on a yawn as he lifted his head. When his eyes blinked open, a drowsy smile spread his lips. For about three seconds. Then the terror Adam had expected took over. He shoved away so hard and so fast he landed on the floor with a loud thud before Adam could gather his wits enough to catch him.

"Bo—"

"Oh crap, oh crap, oh crap." All trace of tiredness left Bo's face. His eyes widened and color stained his cheeks. He crab-walked away from the couch until his back hit the hearth and he scrambled to his feet. "I'm sorry."

Adam pressed to a standing position, snatching Bo's glasses off the back of the couch as he did. "Nothing happened. We just slept. I promise."

Bo nodded like a bobble-head doll and speared both hands into his spiked-up, sleep-mussed hair. Aside from his clear discomfort, Bo was irresistibly adorable fresh out of slumber.

Holding up his hands to indicate the innocence of his intentions, Adam stepped forward and handed Bo his glasses.

Bo accepted them with a shaky hand and eased them up his nose. "Th-thanks."

Sighing, Adam sank onto the couch. He rested his elbows on his knees. "I'm so sorry. This was my fault. I'm the one who put us in that situation. It was unprofessional and unacceptable on every level. If you want to leave, I'll pay you six months' severance and help find you a place to stay on short notice. I can call you a car—"

"You're firing me?" Bo folded his arms in a protective self-hug.

"No." Adam shot to his feet. "No way. I just don't want you to feel obligated to stay here if you're uncomfortable."

Bo was quiet for a minute as he stared Adam down. Eventually he dropped his arms and heaved a weighted sigh. "I'm not exactly innocent either." He licked his lips and lowered his gaze to the floor. "I woke up when you, ah, moved us. So we were lying together."

Adam rolled his shoulders. That meant Bo had been at least somewhat lucid when he'd wrapped those gorgeous limbs around his body. He suppressed a moan. "Okay. We both let it happen. In our own way."

"Yeah." Bo curled his lips in and rubbed an absent hand up and down his bicep. "It wasn't a good idea, though. I mean, okay, yes, I'm attracted to you, and I think you might, maybe, feel the same?" He winced, his gaze darting up. When Adam offered a half smile and nod in confirmation, Bo's shoulders slumped. "Okay. Right. So... we have to get over that."

Laughter barked up Adam's throat. Was he serious? They had to "get over" it? How, exactly? It had already far surpassed any of the physical yearnings he'd experienced before.

Bo was the first man Adam had an interest in who he hadn't simply fucked and forgotten. He was used to satisfying that initial zing of sexual attraction without any thoughts to staying the night, let alone any kind of future with the man. But when his physical urges were left unchecked and he was forced to interact daily with the object of his desire within the close quarters of his own home, things got complicated. Really fuckin' complicated.

Still, despite the confusion muddling his ability to think, he knew Bo was right. They had a professional relationship that couldn't be tainted by all the dirty, sexy things he wanted to do to Bo. To do with Bo.

Hell, they couldn't even do the *un*sexy things his brain kept conjuring up. Like having Sunday brunch and laughing as they reminisced over their adventures the night before. Or curling up on the couch and reading together. Or snuggling in each other's arms for an afternoon nap.

Okay, so that last one was *definitely* off the table. But did the rest of it have to be?

No, it didn't. Maybe they couldn't be lovers—something Adam had never sought before, yet something he couldn't deny wanting from Bo—but who said they couldn't be friends? That'd be the next best thing. Plus, it would be far safer. Adam needed to keep his head in the game so his career didn't find an earlier death than necessary. Friendship he could work around. Anything else? That'd be too risky.

"I'm down for 'getting over' the whole sexual-tension thing." Adam glanced to the stairs and grinned when an idea came to mind. Something he could share with Bo that wouldn't straddle those physical boundaries. Something special they could enjoy together. He angled his eyes back to Bo, who stared at him with a cocked head and pink cheeks. "Can we agree friendship is okay?"

The pink darkened to crimson, but Bo swallowed

and offered a tentative nod. "I'd like that."

"Good." Adam clapped his hands. "First thing on the friendship agenda is another surprise."

When Bo's eyes widened in what could be mock horror but likely held a real trace of the emotion, Adam chuckled. "No need for excessive laundering with this one."

Bo narrowed his gaze. "You swear?"

Adam held up three fingers in the universal Scout's honor oath. "On my life."

"Fine." Bo breathed a heavy, exaggerated sigh. "What's it going to be this time? You don't plan to bust my eardrums again, do you? Because, seriously, you sound like an injured animal when you sing. That kind of auditory torture should be illegal. At the very least, it should come with a warning label so any at-risk parties can come prepared with earplugs."

Adam's jaw dropped. He planted both fists on his hips and shot Bo the stink eye. It took every ounce of willpower he possessed not to bust out laughing. Getting razzed was the last thing he'd expected after their tense wake-up call. But he loved it. "How's about you take your sassy ass into the kitchen and get us some of that go-go-juice-on-a-timer that woke me from a dead sleep this morning. I'll try *really hard* not to burst into spontaneous song while I clean up out here. We'll reconvene at the bottom of the stairs in three minutes. Deal?"

Bo grinned. "Deal."

Adam admired the man's ass as he sashayed toward the kitchen, because, hey, friends could still appreciate the view, right?

As he bent to pick up the throw pillows they'd tossed off the couch, he belted out the opening lyrics of "Hot Patootie, Bless My Soul" from *Rocky Horror*. Complete with Meat Loaf's high-pitched hoot at the beginning.

Bo's head materialized around the corner like a prairie dog popping out of its hole. His hands covered his ears.

"You promised."

Adam shrugged as he tossed the pillows onto the couch. "Be quick with that coffee or I'll sing the extended version. With twice the number of chorus renditions. And a few extra whoops for good measure."

Bo groaned and disappeared into the kitchen. Without missing a beat, Adam picked up where he'd left off. Damn if Bo didn't slide out of the kitchen on his socked feet with two cups of steaming coffee clutched in his hands before Adam could get past the second verse.

"Well, now I know how to get speedy service." Adam nearly busted a gut when Bo's eyes bugged. "I kid, I kid. That wouldn't be fair. Plus, I'm the one paying your health insurance. Wouldn't want our premiums to go up if you wind up needing ear surgery or some shit."

He accepted the mug Bo offered, took a blessed sip of the hot caffeinated liquid, then motioned toward the stairs. "After you. Second door to the right and straight on 'til morning."

"*Peter Pan*? Really?" Bo quirked a brow.

Adam grinned and shrugged. "Wait until you see what's behind that door. Quoting Peter Pan won't seem half so strange once you do."

"No more singing?"

Adam rolled his eyes and bobbed his head in a *yeah, yeah* motion. He pointed to the stairs again. "Go. Or I'll dig into my *Wicked* repertoire. I do a mean Idina Menzel."

Bo let out a squeak and scurried up the steps. Adam enjoyed the view one more time before plastering on a goofy smile and following in his wake.

Chapter Eight

Bo bounded up the stairs, two at a time, and waited for Adam by the door. The grin pulling at Adam's lips when he joined him bordered on ridiculous. It managed to be both childishly adorable and mind-bendingly sexy all at once.

Bo's chest tightened. It wasn't fair. What had he done to deserve the torment of working for—and living with—someone he wanted but couldn't have?

Adam jutted a chin toward the door. "You gonna stand there all day or go inside?"

With a scowl, Bo gave the knob a twist and shoved the door inward. Whatever met him on the other side couldn't be any worse than standing there moping over the future of his sure-to-be-crushed heart.

Except, in a way, it was.

"Oh my God." Bo lifted a hand to cover his gaping mouth as he stepped into the room. No, not just a room, but a *library*. Floor-to-ceiling bookshelves in the same rich mahogany as the one in his bedroom lined every wall. More bookshelves, slightly shorter to allow the warm glow of morning sun to peek over their tops, stood back-to-back to form aisles down the center of the room. A cozy nook with overstuffed leather armchairs, a shared ottoman, and a plethora of colorful throw pillows and fuzzy blankets sat off to the side.

Adam stepped up beside him and folded his arms. His grin had somehow grown in both size and absurdity. "I thought you might like this."

Bo lowered his hand and shook his head. "There must be thousands of books in here. Have you read any of them?"

When Adam quirked a brow, his grin slipping into a wry smirk, Bo gave himself a mental kick to the nuts. Of course he'd read them. Maybe not all, but at least some. He wasn't the brain-dead meathead the media made him out to be. Not by a long shot. "I'm sorry, I didn't mean—"

"It's all good." Adam clapped Bo on the shoulder. "I give off the dumb jock vibe on purpose. It's more intimidating that way. People think I'm stupid enough to do the crazy shit. Keeps 'em on their toes because they never know what to expect."

"Oh. Right." Bo nibbled on his lip and stole another glance to the side. Adam lit up as he scanned the room. His passion for the vast collection was evident, and when those smoky irises shifted to meet Bo's gaze, another punch to the proverbial gut had Bo clutching at his stomach. Why did Adam have to be so perfect?

"Go on, look around. Anything that strikes your fancy is yours for the reading. I've got a little bit of everything. I can't seem to pick a favorite genre, so I read it all." Adam gestured around the room. "It's my guilty pleasure."

Bo frowned. "What is? Reading?"

"Yeah." Adam chuckled. "I never finished high school because my pop pulled me to focus on training. At the time, I thought it was the best thing ever. What hormonal adolescent wouldn't be on board with the idea of doing the thing they love all day instead of going to school? But that doesn't mean I don't like to read and learn new things. I just have to keep that part of me hidden, right alongside my clothes-diva, musical-loving alter ego."

Bo's heart pinched. Adam's father had been the reason he'd left high school early? What kind of parent would place athletics so far above their child's education? It was one thing to drop out of college to pursue a professional sports career, but an entirely different thing to have a parent complicit in the loss of a basic childhood right.

No one deserved to lose the chance to finish high school, and Bo hadn't missed Adam's addition of "at the time." Did he regret the lack of a diploma as much as Bo did?

"I'd say the Beast is more an alter ego than that side of you." Bo tipped his chin and pursed his lips. "It's almost laughable to think of you in that way, now that I know who you really are."

"See?" Adam poked a finger into Bo's chest. A spark of warmth seeped into his skin at the contact. "No one would fear the real me. That's why I gotta keep that dude buried deep."

Bo wandered farther into the room, trailing his fingers over the well-loved spines of countless books. "You've read all of these, haven't you?"

"Nah. Not all of them." Adam mimicked Bo's absent tracing, stopping short of where Bo's fingers still rested. Bo itched to feel the warmth and comfort of Adam's touch again, but as if reading his mind, Adam dropped his hand and stepped away. "I've read quite a few, but not all. Those I haven't read are here because I hope to someday."

Bo wrung his hands to dispel the urge to reach out for Adam's. Instead, he continued his trek through the rows of books, marveling that several of the titles had brothers on his own shelf down the hall. "You've got good taste, Mr. Littrell."

"Hey, what'd I tell ya about that 'Mr.' shit?" Adam winked when Bo shot him a look. "I'm kidding. You can call me whatever you want."

Bo chewed back a moan and gripped his shoulders in a self-hug. Memories of lying in Adam's arms swirled through his brain. He'd barely caught himself from spilling an inappropriate term of endearment when he'd woken pressed against that hard body, encircled by the solid warmth of that strong embrace.

He bit his lip until the tang of coppery blood hit his tongue. It was time to change the subject. "Have you ever thought of going back to get your GED?"

Adam guffawed. "I'm nearly forty. It's a bit too late for that."

"It's never too late." Bo turned on his heel to face Adam head-on. "I never finished high school either, and you can bet your butt I'll get my GED the first chance I find. Even if I *am* forty."

Rather than firing off another flippant response, Adam squinted his eyes. He swiped his thumb over his lower lip and followed the same path with his tongue. The action drew Bo's gaze to that plump, kissable mouth. His balls tightened.

"You didn't finish high school either?"

Bo swallowed and worked his jaw back and forth. Admitting to his lack of education wasn't something he made a habit of, but Adam wouldn't judge him. Not because he shared the same deficiency, but because he was a good man. Bo trusted that now more than ever. "My dad passed away when my sister Lulu was only eleven. I was eighteen, so I took custody. My priorities shifted after that. No way I'd let Lulu end up in the system when I could take care of her myself."

"And taking care of her meant quitting school so

you could work?" Adam's voice lowered an octave, and he frowned. "I'm not sure I could ever do something that self-less."

Bo laughed. "You could. Trust me, you could. If someone you loved suddenly relied on you for their very existence, you'd give up everything to make sure they never wanted for anything. I don't regret quitting school because I did it for Lulu. She's my whole world."

Adam's frown softened into a flat-lipped smile. "But you'd go back and finish if you could."

"Heck yeah." Was that really a question? "I fully intend to. Some day."

Nodding, Adam ran a hand through his cropped hair. "I've got a proposal for you."

A nervous chuckle slipped past Bo's lips. No way the proposal Adam had in mind would mirror the one Bo wanted to hear. Inappropriate or not. "Ah, okay."

"Retirement's looming in my future. Having my high school diploma might prove beneficial, especially considering I have no fuckin' clue what I'm going to do with my life when I can't fight anymore." Adam shrugged and offered a lopsided grin. "I'm an old man. The thought of going back to school terrifies me. Any chance you'd be interested in doing it with me? I could use the support. I doubt I'll ever do it on my own."

If Adam had grown a second head, Bo wouldn't have been more surprised. He closed his gaping mouth with a clash of teeth and pressed his lips together to keep it shut. Was Adam really offering him a chance to get his GED? With guaranteed time to study because he'd be doing it alongside Adam? "Ah...."

What the heck was he supposed to say? He had no clue how much it would cost. Did he have the funds? Lulu's education took priority over his own. He couldn't risk running out of money. His budget was already tight.

"Tell you what, don't decide now. Do some research

for us. See what it'll take to get enrolled or whatever we've gotta do." Adam slapped a palm against the solid wood of the nearest bookshelf. "If you're willing to help, consider the tuition costs a perk of the job. You'd be doing me a favor, after all."

Bo was shaking his head before Adam finished speaking. "No way. If I do this, I'll pay my own way."

Rumbling laughter filled the air, and Adam waggled his brows. "You have no idea how much work I'll be. Trust me, it'll be compensation well earned."

When Bo shook his head again, Adam landed a hand on his shoulder and squeezed. "Dude, I'll be a huge thorn in your side. Think about how much effort it takes to wake my ass up in the morning and multiply that by, like, fifty. At least. You deserve a little extra for the pain and suffering."

Bo groaned and raised a dramatic hand to his forehead. "You're not doing a great job of selling the idea."

Adam snorted. "You can always say no. But if I don't have studying to keep me occupied while I wait for the training camp to start, I might have to take Kyle up on those singing lessons he suggested. Which would mean practicing at home. A lot. Like, all the time. Night and day. Day and night."

"Okay, okay, okay." Bo couldn't hold in the laughter, especially when Adam grinned like a loon when he did. He wasn't *that* bad of a singer. In fact, the deep bass rumble of Adam's voice did indecent things to Bo's body and brain alike. Especially when he wasn't actively trying to sound like a drowning cat. "I'll do it."

"And you'll let me pay?"

Bo sighed. His heart did an extra little flip. If the masses had any clue how sweet and wonderful the *real* Beast was, he'd be fending off suitors with a stick. Or he'd be married. Or, if nothing else, his bed wouldn't be empty every night, as it had been the past week.

The sinking weight of jealousy tugged at Bo's belly.

That was a reality that wouldn't last and one he'd have to learn to live with. Even if Adam had shown a return interest in Bo, it would be short-lived now they'd secured the label of friendship around whatever the heck this was between them.

Once Adam moved on, his infamous slew of fast-and-dirty affairs would kick back into full gear. And when they did? Bo would have to sleep two doors down with a pillow over his head while Adam gave other men the things he wanted.

He scowled. Life was so totally unfair.

Chapter Nine

Adam's gym shoes slapped against the mechanical belt of his treadmill, his thoughts spinning and twisting nearly as fast as the gears powering the machine beneath him.

What the hell had he been thinking? Since when did he want to get his GED? Since never, that's when. Especially not now. His training camp for the title defense fight that would determine his future in the UFC was only a few months away. He needed to focus on getting his body ready, not wasting precious hours studying for some damn piece of paper that didn't mean shit to him or his career.

But he'd sensed the yearning in Bo. That paper meant something to him. Over the past week, Adam had learned enough about Bo to guess it wouldn't be a simple task to offer him a gift. Even if the gift were as minimal as the cost and time it would take to study and prepare for the GED.

So he'd stretched the truth a bit and asked Bo to help him chase a dream that wasn't his own. The way those brilliant green eyes had lit up when he finally agreed was all the payment Adam needed.

Plus, the endeavor might harbor a few additional benefits. It would give Adam some guaranteed time with Bo where they wouldn't be acting as boss and employee. After their conversation that morning solidifying the impossibility of a physical relationship, he didn't want to risk losing the chance at friendship.

If he couldn't have Bo in his bed, he'd damn well make sure he could at least have him as a friend. There was something about the man. He drove Adam to distraction. Even now, with a runner's high that usually kept his attention focused on pushing his physical limits, Adam couldn't keep his mind on the task at hand.

All he could think about was Bo's sweet smile and that spark of passion when he spoke about his sister and his dreams to finish his education. How hard had that been to lose his father at such a young age? And with a little sister to look after and support through the traumatic aftermath, no less.

Bo had been the only person standing between Lulu and the terrifying foster care system. And yet he'd been a kid himself, hadn't he? Still in high school. Forced to give up his childhood to enter the workforce so he could take care of his sister. But when he talked about it all, there was nothing but love holding up his words.

He had the kindest soul and purest heart Adam had ever known. Bo was as courageous as he was brilliant and loving. Was it such a shock Adam wanted more than a business relationship with him?

"I thought Sundays were your day of rest."

The tenor of Bo's voice rose above the EDM track blaring over the gym speakers. Adam startled at the unexpected interruption but couldn't stop his grin. He slammed the heel of his palm on the Stop button and hopped to the side rails as the belt jerked to a halt.

"You didn't have to quit running. I'm sorry." Bo stood inside the door to Adam's home gym. He clutched a notebook, his eyes bugging behind his glasses. "I shouldn't have bothered you."

The irrational joy at seeing Bo should have worried Adam. They'd only left each other a few short hours before. But it didn't. He was too old and too experienced to fight the inevitable. He'd settle for friendship because that was all they could have, but his feelings for Bo weren't going away anytime soon. Plus, friends could have the total hots for each other as long as they didn't act on it.

When Adam caught Bo's eyes wandering over his shirtless torso and settling on the bulge at the front of his gym shorts, his grin spread even wider. At least he wasn't suffering alone.

"You aren't bothering me at all." Adam snatched his towel off the handrail of the treadmill and ran it over his sweat-drenched chest. Bo licked his lips, swallowed, and darted his gaze away. Adam's shoulders drew back on a ridiculous swell of pride. He worked damn hard to keep his body in shape and was used to others appreciating his physique as part of the public-image package. But there was something special about Bo's reaction. Whether they could act on it or not, there was a comfort in knowing the attraction went both ways.

Adam threw the towel over his shoulder and sauntered over to where Bo stood frozen by the door. "Whatcha got there?"

When Bo blinked up at him with those big, beautiful eyes, Adam's knees went weak. Had to be his age. Maybe he *was* getting too old for this shit.

But no, it was more than that. Bo's lips tilted into a crooked smile, and Adam's stomach dropped to share space with his wobbly knees. Yeah, it had to do with a lot more than his age.

Beauregard Wilkins would be the death of him far

before age took its toll.

"I, ah, did some research on the GED." Bo bit his lip as he held the notebook out for Adam to see. Scribbled notes covered the page in the big, looping penmanship Adam already associated with Bo. "They offer testing every other weekend. There are classes we could take if you want, or we could self-teach. They have loads of materials available. And if we go that route, it's estimated we should be ready within a couple of months. As long as we spend a few evenings a week studying."

A few evenings a week. Adam inwardly cringed but kept his face neutral. He still had a little over two months until training camp started. He could skip a couple two-a-days for Bo's sake. He'd spend a few more hours on his evening workouts the rest of the week to make up for it. Totally doable.

"Let's do it. Get us whatever we need, and we can start tomorrow." Adam ran the towel over his damp neck. He tilted his chin when Bo bobbed his head in agreement but didn't disappear as he'd expected. "Something else on your mind?"

Bo's gaze snapped to Adam's, and an adorable pink blushed his cheeks. "Ah, no."

"You sure?" Adam scratched his thumb over an eyebrow. "You aren't bothering me in the least. If you need or want something, I'm here. I can take a break or even call it for the night. No biggie."

Bo worked his pursed lips side to side before dropping them into a pout. "Would it be okay if I maybe came in here every so often? I promise I won't get under your feet while you're using it, and I won't shirk my duties—"

"Dude, of course." Adam laughed. He'd love nothing more than to have Bo share this space with him. "You won't be 'under my feet.' Why don't you join me in the evenings? I hate working out alone. You'd be doing me a favor."

The narrow-eyed skepticism pinching Bo's face was downright adorable. He folded his arms over his notebook and plumped out one of those kissably delicious lips. "I haven't been in a gym since junior year. I have no clue what I'm doing. Trust me, I'll get in your way."

A thrill raced up Adam's spine. He loved a good challenge, and one of his favorite things to do before his fame had gotten in the way of his regular life had been to help others train. There was something satisfying about guiding someone through the routines his own body craved, especially when he got to stick around long enough to see the other person grow to love the activities as much as he did.

"Tell you what, how about we work out together? As in, I'll spot you, you spot me, and I can teach you as we go. I kinda get off on training people. Probably has something to do with a subconscious boost to my ego or some shit, but you'll be exactly opposite of getting in my way. Having a partner can be motivating. It's also a whole helluva lot easier."

Bo rocked on his heels and nibbled on his lip in much the same way Adam had imagined doing. Repeatedly.

"I'm a string bean, and you're... well, you're a beast." Bo snorted out an awkward laugh. The pink in his cheeks turned crimson. "You could probably bench press me with one arm, all while I'm holding the heaviest weights I can manage to lift two-handed. I'll hold you back."

A challenge indeed. Adam pointed to a table near the door that held bottled water and a basket with clean, folded towels Bo himself kept laundered and stocked. "Leave your notebook there, and give me a chance to show you what I mean. I promise, if you're 'getting in the way,' I'll let you know."

Bo didn't look convinced, but he swallowed and did as Adam asked. He glanced at his jeans, T-shirt, and worn gym shoes, then knit his brow. "Should I change first?"

The temptation to suggest Bo strip to his underwear

nearly won over Adam's good senses. The mental image it produced had him shifting on his feet and sending *down, boy* vibes to his cock.

"We won't do anything too exciting this go-round. I was getting close to wrapping for the evening, anyway. Next time, you can come prepared."

"Okay." Bo licked his lips. "So, ah, where do you want me?"

No amount of internal scolding could contain Adam's response to those words. He turned his hips to hide the growing proof of his filthy-minded attraction and pretended his movement had been altruistic by pointing to the treadmill. "Since it's your first time getting active in a while, let's start with a warm-up walk."

Bo scampered to the machine and hopped on. The excitement radiating off him was near-palpable. He stood on the belt and stared at the electronic console with a puzzled scrunch of his brow. "How the heck does this thing work?"

When Bo pressed the quick-start button before Adam could tell him not to, the belt jerked to life and he tumbled face-first into the cup holder. A bout of contagious laughter rolled through the room rather than the cry of pain Adam had feared.

After adjusting his shorts to camouflage his erection, Adam climbed onto the elliptical beside Bo. He walked him through setting up an easy warm-up routine, then swallowed a groan when Bo shot him a toothy grin and puffed out his chest.

This would be a challenge, all right. A challenge to keep his dick under control.

Tomorrow he'd wear a pair of compression shorts under his baggier pair. It wouldn't solve all his problems, but at least it would help. Somewhat.

Bo shifted his walk to a swagger. He sashayed his hips and tossed a wink over his shoulder.

Fuck.
Or maybe it wouldn't do shit.

Chapter Ten

66Hey, Grandpa, how goes it?"

The laughter lacing Adam's words should've brought a glare to Bo's face, but even those muscles were sore. It was easier to grunt than to risk any unnecessary physical movement.

Adam flopped on the couch at Bo's feet with all the lithe agility of a man who hadn't spearheaded a murderous workout routine the night before. Or spent another three hours at the gym this morning. Yet somehow, he had. Without showing the slightest sign of discomfort or negative ramifications.

Just... *how*?

"I bet you'll listen to me next time, won't you, young grasshopper?" Adam pulled a knee onto the couch so he could face Bo and grinned with an unnecessarily boisterous gusto. "Especially considering the soreness is always worse on day two. This ain't nothin' compared to what you're gonna face tomorrow."

Bo moaned. How was that physically possible? He'd never hurt so bad in his life. How could it get any worse?

He wanted to kick his own backside from here to Alaska for his idiocy. Adam *had* tried to talk him out of pushing things as hard as he had. But after that first night, where Adam had him walk on a treadmill for twenty minutes and called it quits, he'd wanted to prove he didn't need coddling. If he was going to join Adam in his workouts, he didn't want to embarrass himself. Worse, he didn't want to hinder Adam's ability to get in the workout he needed. After all, keeping his body fit was Adam's full-time job.

Like it was Bo's full-time job to do about anything other than lie around on his boss's couch like a sack full of bruised potatoes. He struggled to lean on his elbows and worked up a good glower. "Listen, meathead, it isn't nice to tease the wounded."

"Meathead?" Adam's brows popped. "Ouch. Do you talk to your baby sister with that mouth?"

Bo whimpered as he pushed to a full upright sitting position. "Actually, I do. Hence the term 'meathead' rather than something more colorful."

Faced with raising an adolescent when he had still been one himself had meant a lot of adjustments and a crash course in maturity. Which wasn't something Bo was entirely new to. His mother had been diagnosed with stage IV cervical cancer early in her pregnancy with Lulu and decided to postpone treatment until her daughter was born. It'd resulted in a healthy baby girl, but their mother had passed a few short weeks later.

His family had already been battling financial difficulties before her death, so Bo's father had to take on two full-time jobs to keep them afloat. Even then, there weren't enough funds available to pay for evening and overnight childcare. At seven years old, Bo had already been Lulu's primary caregiver.

"Hold the phone." Adam tilted his head. "You're

saying you *never* curse? Like, not ever?"

"I had impressionable little ears looking to me as an example. I learned other ways to vent my frustrations. Ways that wouldn't get me pulled in for a parent-teacher conference because the mouth attached to those ears chose to repeat what they'd heard."

Adam huffed out a laugh. "I've got thirteen years on you, and you're more grown-up than I'll ever be."

Before Bo could respond, the doorbell echoed through the living space and Adam leapt to his feet. He gave Bo's shoulder a squeeze on his way to the door. "Kyle's here to talk shop. He was also tasked with dinner provisions. Cross every appendage you have that he didn't cook it himself or we'll be going hungry tonight."

Bo labored to his feet and met Adam and Kyle in the kitchen. Adam scowled as he peered into a reusable insulated shopping bag. On the other side of the room, Kyle lounged against the counter with a Cheshire cat grin in place.

"What the hell is this shit?" Adam poked a finger into the bag. He pulled his arm back a second later as if something had bitten him. "It's spongy. Why is it spongy?"

"It's tripe, you big baby. It's good for you. Lots of protein."

"Tripe?" Adam screwed up his face. "Da fuck is tripe?"

"It's the lining of an animal's stomach. In this instance, a cow's." Kyle's deep laughter rolled through the room when Adam's eyes widened. Bo couldn't help but join him.

"Count me out." Adam shoved the bag away and folded his arms, grumbling under his breath as he glared between Bo and Kyle. "Glad you assholes think my suffering is amusing. If I pass out from starvation later, you're both fired."

A tingle of unease raced up Bo's spine but dissipated

into something far more debauched when Adam shot him a wink and made a show of stomping over to the refrigerator and tugging it open.

Kyle angled a look at Bo. He waggled his brows, shoved off the counter, and descended on Adam's turned back. A high-pitched peal of laughter preceded a flash of movement. Almost quicker than Bo could process the sight, Adam had Kyle pinned to the tile floor.

Jealousy sizzled under Bo's skin like the heated jolt of a frayed low-voltage wire. He'd give about anything to have Adam straddle him that way. If even for a moment.

Maybe he should take note and test out Adam's tickle spots sometime?

The thought of running his fingers over that hard flank of muscle had Bo shifting on his feet. His sore body ached as he did, and he welcomed the distraction. Tickling his boss was on the no-go list. As was even the thought of touching him. Anywhere. Ever.

"Bo, I know we're not at the 'I'll help you bury the body' stage of our relationship, but have we at least reached 'feign ignorance'?" Adam grunted when Kyle bucked beneath him. He repositioned so his body covered Kyle's, did some sort of scissor-kick with his legs, and three seconds later, Kyle was on his stomach with both arms trapped behind his back. "Because there's a distinct possibility I'm gonna murder this son of a bitch."

Hearing Adam insinuate they were at *any* stage of a relationship sent a giddy wave through Bo's belly. He grinned. "My loyalties are with you, boss. Just tell me where to find the shovel."

"Hey, I'm the one who got you this job, Wilkins." Kyle's voice was muffled and came out on a wheeze when Adam shifted his bulk higher up the man's back. "You can both thank me later. I expect an invite to the wedding."

Thank him? For what? And whose wedding? Before Bo could question the bizarre statements, Adam growled and twisted one of Kyle's arms until it looked almost broken.

"Jesus fuckin' Christ, man, uncle. *Uncle.*"

Adam released Kyle and sprang to his feet with an incomprehensible sprightliness. He held out a hand and yanked the older man upright, giving him one of those back-slapping, one-armed guy hugs before shooting a cheesy grin Bo's direction. "I dunno about you, dude, but I'm not eating spongy cow innards. Whataya say to a little Grubhub delivery?"

"Sold." Bo slipped his phone out of his back pocket and pulled out the closest barstool. When he climbed on, the overworked muscles in his butt screamed, and he winced at the injustice.

Kyle guffawed and jabbed an elbow into Adam's ribs. "And you said my plan didn't work. Looks like you found some time for fun, after all."

"For fuck's sake, asshole." Adam turned cherry red, his eyes flashing a dangerous stormy gray. "Bo's sore because he's been working out with me. That's it. Leave it alone."

"Huh." Kyle's twinkling eyes shifted to meet Bo's. "So, you've got him going back for his GED *and* you're keeping his grumpy old bear ass company in the gym? You're an angel, Wilkins."

Bo's overcharged brain zeroed in on the words "bare ass," and a whimper caught in his throat. The visual that supplied almost overrode all other thought. *Almost.* He might be young and uneducated, but he wasn't stupid. He'd gotten the gist of their conversation.

He wasn't sure what plan Kyle referred to, but he was pretty sure it involved his backside being sore for a much more enjoyable reason than overexertion in the gym.

Why was life so frickin' unfair? He and Adam clearly wanted the same things, yet they weren't allowed to have them. If it weren't for his drive to give Lulu the best future possible, something he'd be putting at risk by even considering such a thing, Bo would jump to his feet and kiss Adam senseless. Sore muscles and Kyle's presence be damned.

Unfortunately, that wasn't possible. Neither were any of the other endless fantasies he'd conjured up over the past week and a half.

Sighing, Bo offered Kyle the best smile he could muster. "I'm not an angel, Mr. Bryant. I'm a dedicated employee. That's all."

When Adam hung his head and shoved his hands into the pockets of his jeans, Bo's heart twisted. Maybe someday they could be the *more* they both wanted.

Maybe. Someday.

Chapter Eleven

*A*dam scrubbed both hands over his face and stifled a groan. He glanced at Bo, who sat on the floor opposite him at the stone coffee table, frowning at the workbooks spread before him. His pencil tapped in an irritated rhythm against the pages.

Everything about Bo's concentration and drive to succeed during this grueling cram session drove Adam to the brink of insanity. Not out of jealousy, even though his own abilities paled in comparison to Bo's, but because his passion, resilience, and dedication were so goddamn sexy.

Over the past month, Bo had blossomed under the stress that weighed Adam down. His excitement was palpable. It lit up the room and lifted Adam's spirits unlike anything else. Anytime he wanted to give up, one look at Bo would ease his frustrations and remind him why he'd committed to this in the first place.

Because it meant the world to Bo.

"You feeling as fried as I am?"

Bo's frown deepened into a scowl. He dropped his pencil and met Adam's stare. "Who cares how much Jack spent on his new car? And why does it matter that it was $2,400 less than five times the $5,000 selling price of his old one? What benefit does the ability to figure this out provide for my future?"

Chuckling, Adam tucked his thumb under the cover of his book and flipped it closed. Getting his GED might be a dream come true for Bo, but that didn't mean he was immune to the stress. He just handled it better than Adam because it came with a prize at the end. One that meant much more to Bo.

"I'm sure they'd say all this 'knowledge' adds to our critical thinking skills or some shit like that."

"I don't think my critical thinking skills have any more room to grow. I'm at capacity." Bo moaned and let his forehead drop to the table. "I'm too old to learn high school math. My brain doesn't work that way anymore."

The mutual teasing about the gap in their age hadn't let up with time. In fact, as they grew more comfortable together, the razzing only increased. There was no doubt Bo's remark had been meant as a proverbial jab to his elderly ribs.

Adam stretched his leg under the table and gave Bo's bent knee a shove with his foot. "Watch it with the 'too old' comments, pipsqueak. How do you think I feel? At least you've been helping Lulu with her homework all these years. Keeping your exposure level up. The last time I gave any of this shit a second thought, you were still in diapers."

"I was not." Bo's head whipped up and his eyes flashed with mock indignation. "Are you trying to say I was still wetting my pants at six years old?"

A bark of laughter rose up Adam's throat. "Your addition's a little off there, Einstein. By your calculations, I was taking freshman math at nineteen."

"Nuh-uh. You would've been fourteen or fifteen.

Which means I would've been...." Bo tapped his pencil against the thick black upper frame of his browline glasses. His head tilted as his clearly overmathed brain struggled to work out the simple equation.

"If I was fifteen, you would've been at the terrible-two stage. As stubborn as you are, I bet your folks knew better than to try and potty train you early. So, yes, my guess is you were definitely still pissing your pants the last time I did high school algebra."

Bo's jaw sagged. His mouth opened and closed a few times as his brows drew together. "Jeez. You really *are* old."

Before Adam could retort with an exaggerated show of offense, Bo shot him one of his patented belly-twisting, heart-stopping grins. Adam huffed out a calming breath to get himself under control before returning the smile. "Whataya say we call it quits a bit early tonight? We're a month into this miserable shit. Halfway done. I'd say that calls for a celebration."

"A celebration?" Bo squinted his eyes. "I need more information before I agree to anything. You're a man who can't be trusted with surprises."

Adam let his wrist go limp before pointing to his chest. He popped his brows and drew back his chin in faux shock. "Who, me?"

"Yes, you." Bo glowered. "If you aren't ruining my beautiful new clothes with sticky fake blood, you're assaulting my ears with crappy music, or landing me on the wrong side of a grumpy bouncer. My tailbone is still bruised from that behemoth throwing me out on my backside."

Guilt pinched Adam's stomach. He hadn't meant for Bo to get tossed out of his favorite club the previous weekend. He was so used to waltzing through the entrance of 1 OAK at the Mirage unchecked—the velvet rope lifted and his path cleared without question—that he hadn't considered his tagalong would warrant different treatment.

It had been meant as a surprise, so he hadn't told Bo

where they were going that night. The goal was to show him the glitz and glam of the Vegas Strip, one favorite haunt at a time. But Bo had forgotten his ID. The bouncer didn't catch up with them until Adam was already at the bar ordering drinks, and because Bo could easily pass for underage in the dim kaleidoscopic lighting, he'd been thrown out on his ass before Adam even knew he was missing.

"Okay, okay, fine." Adam harrumphed. "No surprises. How about plain old dinner? We could hit up Giada for old time's sake."

Bo slammed his workbook shut and smirked. "I'm game, but only if there's no fake blood in my immediate future."

Adam held up his trusty three-finger Boy Scout salute. "On my honor."

"I should get my head examined for trusting a curmudgeon like you not to tell a lie." Rolling his eyes, Bo rose to his feet. "Come on, old man. Let's get some food."

As always, Giada was hopping. The host recognized Adam and made quick work of finding them a table, although the location was less than optimal. It sat smack dab in the middle of five others and held no semblance of privacy.

"Any chance we could wait for a booth in the back?" Adam side-eyed a group of twentysomethings sharing a meal a few feet from the two-top the host had led them to. One of the young men had narrowed his gaze on Adam and was whispering to the guy beside him. He'd been made. "We don't mind sitting at the bar for a bit."

"Nonsense." The host pulled out the chair closest to Bo and smiled as he gestured for him to sit. "Ms. De Laurentiis would be upset if I didn't seat you immediately. This is one of our finest tables, Mr. Littrell. It offers a prime view."

Not wishing to make a scene, Adam nodded and thanked the host. Bo joined him at the table when he sat, oblivious to Adam's concern.

Bo's teeth raked over his lip as he scanned the menu. "So are you going to get the same thing you got last time? Or try something new?"

"I've had everything on the menu at least twice. It's all phenomenal."

Adam smiled when Bo's expression turned serious and contemplative. No doubt he was attempting mental calculations with his overworked brain to assess his financial situation. Adam had learned to be careful when they went out to eat together so as not to hurt Bo's wallet if he couldn't convince the man to let him pay. This time, considering the restaurant he'd chosen, Bo would just have to bend. "This was my idea, so I'm footing the bill. You know the rules. Order whatever you want."

Bo opened his mouth to argue—an inevitability Adam found as adorable as it was infuriating—but before he could get a word out, the two young men who had recognized Adam appeared at their table. Bo cocked his head in silent question when Adam's face slipped into the hardened countenance of the Beast.

"Holy shit. I knew I was right. You're really him, aren't you? You're the Beast." The towheaded, pimple-faced man who had first spotted Adam bounced on his heels. "I'm a huge fan, man. You're a fuckin' *legend*."

The second guy, nearly half a foot shorter than his lanky fellow, ran a hand through his dark brown locks and shoved his friend aside. He flashed a brilliant white smile as he cocked a hip against the table, blocking both Bo and the blond from Adam's view. "We've met before. At an after-party following one of your title defenses a few years ago. Do you remember me? My name's Rajesh. We had a hot encounter on the balcony of the L Suite at Mandalay

Bay. You were going to take me home with you, but we got separated."

Oh, for fuck's sake. Adam clenched his jaw and glared at the beaming, cocky man leaning way too far into his personal space. No, he didn't remember the guy. But that wasn't saying much. How many "hot encounters" had he had on random balconies over the years? More than he could count. Not that he was proud of that fact. Especially not now. Not with Bo sitting two feet away. "Can't say I do."

Rajesh's grin only grew at that response. "Oh, sure you do. You're playing coy because you've got a date. But I could do you way better than this twink ever could. And I don't require dinner first. Why don't you take me back to your place? I can show you what a good time looks like."

A month ago, Adam would've taken Rajesh up on that offer without thinking twice, but he never would've brought him home—that line of his story was utter bullshit. Rajesh was clearly lying. At least partially. Adam never brought sexual partners to his house. That was his sanctuary, and he didn't do overnights.

But now? Things had changed. He wasn't interested in some random one-night stand. His priorities had shifted. He wasn't sure when, but he damn well knew why.

Beauregard Wilkins. That's why.

Adam slammed his fist on the table. Cutlery and glass clinked as the wooden surface vibrated beneath his attack.

Rajesh pushed to a full standing position, a smirk tugging at his lips. "There's my sexy Beast. Come on, honey, blow off this little bitch and let a real man take you to bed."

"Fuck off, you—"

A very deliberate clearing of the throat drew Adam's fuming gaze to the host, whose eyes glimmered with nervous anxiety. "S-sir? Is there a problem here?"

"Yeah, there's a fucking problem." Adam pointed at

Rajesh. "You have ten seconds to get this piece of shit out of my sight before I pound his ass into the ground."

Rather than scampering away as any smart human would've done, Rajesh blew Adam a kiss. "For your sake, I hope your little twink puts out. If he doesn't, I'm staying at the Flamingo. Room 416." He linked arms with the wide-eyed blond, sneered at the host, and sauntered out of the restaurant.

Bo sat like a statue, his lips curled in and his eyes bugging behind the rims of his glasses.

If there had ever been a chance Bo might give Adam a shot someday, it was gone now.

Just. Fuckin'. Great.

Chapter Twelve

Bo shifted his hips, hoping to make room in the tight-fitting designer jeans for his unexpected response to Adam's beastly nature. At first he'd found the whole encounter amusing. Adam's player reputation was hardly top-secret information. It was a wonder they hadn't run into more of his prior conquests over the past month.

But when things started to heat up and Rajesh the Stupid kept poking the proverbial bear with his idiotic goading, the humor died. Not because Bo was offended by the insinuation he was after Adam or that he'd fail at pleasing him in bed—in their own way, those were both true, after all—but because he'd gotten his first real look at the man the media feared.

And the Beast, in all his glory, was sexy as all get-out.

Adam scrubbed both hands over his face, a low growl rumbling up his throat. "Fuck, Bo, I'm so sorry."

"There's nothing to be sorry about." Bo tried to offer a smile of reassurance, but Adam wouldn't meet his eye. "It isn't your fault—"

A high-pitched squeal assaulted Bo's eardrums. He cringed away from the noise. Across the table, Adam's eyes darkened. "We gotta get outta here. Now."

Bo opened his mouth to ask why, but Adam was already on his feet. He grabbed Bo's bicep and yanked him out of his seat. Bo tripped over his feet as he attempted to make his legs go from a dead standstill to near-running after Adam.

The squawking and screaming grew louder as they neared the entrance, and bright flashes of light now paired with the auditory attack.

"Shit." Adam stopped abruptly. Bo continued blundering forward, but because Adam still gripped his arm, his momentum carried him in a wide, stumbling arc. When he crashed into Adam's chest, Adam wrapped an arm around Bo's waist to steady him. The cacophony grew near-deafening.

"Mr. Littrell, sir, there's a back door off the kitchen." The host's quavering voice appeared out of nowhere. "I've already got an Uber en route. Should be here momentarily. The gentleman promises to be discreet."

Rather than releasing Bo or shoving him away, Adam tucked him against his side. The hard warmth of his body felt like heaven, and the problem in Bo's pants kicked back to life in earnest. He should be afraid, or at the very least concerned, but with Adam holding him close, he felt nothing but safe.

Adam led him through the kitchen, but all Bo caught were glimpses of chrome and harsh fluorescent light. Most of his attention focused on the solid security of Adam's arm around his shoulders and the sinew and muscle moving against his side, separated by only a few thin layers of clothing.

By the time they exited the building, the Uber driver was waiting for them. Adam hustled Bo inside, then slipped in beside him. He gave the driver his address, then dropped his head against the seat back and blew out a long, low breath. "Well, that was a clusterfuck. Stupid asshole went out and ran his mouth. I could wring his neck."

Bo rubbed at the spot on his shoulder where Adam's strong hand had gripped him only a few moments before. He bit his lip to stop the frustration and loss from pulling his mouth into a pout. He didn't want to talk about Adam's ex whatever he was. Not right then. Not when he could still feel Adam's body surrounding him. Holding him close. Keeping him protected. "What are we going to do about your car? It's still parked in the garage."

Adam chuckled, rolling his head on the seat until he met Bo's gaze. "We can pick it up tomorrow. Or I'll pay someone to drive it out to the house. It's not a big deal."

Maybe to Adam it wasn't. But Bo was responsible for the car, even if Adam did more than half the driving. It was part of his job. He glanced out the window. As per usual, traffic on the Strip crawled by. They'd barely made it half a block. "Why don't I hop out and go get it now? It's a short walk, and it wasn't me that crowd was after."

"No fuckin' way." Adam sat up straight, his hand landing on Bo's knee. Another physical touch that would haunt Bo in his bed that night. "They saw you with me. They took your picture. It isn't safe. You aren't going anywhere but home with me."

A tingle raced under Bo's skin like the jolt of a live wire, and his insolent dick stirred yet again. He lived with Adam, but it wasn't his home. He couldn't think of it that way. He had to keep their professional relationship at the forefront of his mind, even if they had developed a friendship over the past weeks. A friendship so symbiotic and perfect it made keeping his feelings under check much, much more difficult.

He needed to change the subject.

"Why do you hide behind the Beast when you're in public?"

Adam tipped his chin as he studied Bo. A slow, wry smile crept up his lips, and he huffed out a laugh. His hand disappeared off Bo's knee as he settled back into the seat. "A clothes diva who loves musicals and cries at sappy romance movies wouldn't intimidate the badass motherfuckers I gotta face in the octagon. I've told you that."

"But you aren't facing any, ah, bad you-know-what's at restaurants. Or on the street. So why hide your wonderful personality?" Bo stifled a grin when Adam's cheeks flushed a glorious shade of pink. "It's got to be lonely pretending to be someone you aren't all the time. How can you develop relationships with people when they don't know who you are?"

Adam was quiet a moment, then a half smile pulled at the corner of his lips. "You know who I am."

Holy crap on a cracker. Bo swallowed and shifted his hips. This conversation was doing jack-nothing for his ever-present erection. "I do, and we're friends because of it. Can you imagine how many other friends you'd have if you let people in more often? And not only friends but, you know, other things too."

"Other things?" Adam lifted a brow.

Bo pressed his lips flat. There was no doubt Adam knew exactly what he was getting at. "Yeah, you know, people you could hang out with who aren't me. Or Kyle. People who could, ah, do the things with you we can't."

Adam ran his tongue in a slow, deliberate circle around the point of a canine. "And what things can't you do with me?"

An exasperated, horny groan escaped Bo's throat. "You know what I mean."

"Clearly, I don't. Enlighten me."

Heat flooded Bo's cheeks even as it crept into his

groin. His dick throbbed, and he clenched his fists. He'd never wanted another man more than he wanted Adam. Sleeping two doors down from the star of every sexual fantasy his brain could conjure was pure torture. As was spending his waking hours in even closer proximity. Especially when Adam was half-naked and covered in sweat 50 percent of the time.

But wanting was a far stretch from being allowed. And he absolutely was *not* allowed to carry through on his desires. Not with his boss. Not with Lulu's next tuition payment coming up.

Bo ordered his fists to loosen, then smoothed his hands over his thighs and cleared his throat. "You know... b-boyfriend stuff."

Dang it. Stuttering was exactly opposite of what he needed to be doing. He needed to give off an aura of nonchalance. He needed Adam to believe he didn't *want* "boyfriend stuff."

"Boyfriend stuff?" Adam's eyes flashed with delight. At Bo's obvious discomfort, no doubt.

Bo folded his arms and narrowed his gaze. "Are you going to parrot everything I say?"

Adam lifted his hands in innocence. "Hey, sorry, I'm trying to follow what you mean. I've never done the boyfriend thing, so I'm gonna need a bit more clarification on what this 'boyfriend stuff' entails."

"You are such a pain in my butt." Bo glowered at Adam. "You know exactly what I mean. I'm not going to say it, especially because *it* is off-limits."

Adam sobered. His face slipped into a scowl. "I'm sorry about Rajesh. I've done a lot of things I'm not proud of, and he's one of them. But I've changed. I'm not like that anymore. I don't want the same things I used to want."

What was Adam getting at? He couldn't possibly be trying to say that he, what, wanted "boyfriend stuff" now? No frickin' way. That wasn't the Beast's style. And even if

it was, it didn't matter. Lulu's well-being came before anything. Even if Bo worked three full-time jobs, he'd never
make the kind of money Adam paid.

"You don't have to explain yourself to me." Bo
huffed out a breath. "I'm just your PA."

"Right. I know. I'm sorry." Adam shrunk into the
corner and cast his gaze to the blurred landscape beyond
his window. The look of resignation marring his beautiful
features stopped Bo's heart cold.

"Your PA... and your friend. I'm your friend too,
Adam."

Adam nodded, a weak smile ghosting over his lips.
But his stare never left the rhythmic pulse of the passing
streetlights.

Bo's heart kicked sluggishly back to life, but the damage was already done. His chest ached and nausea coiled in
his gut.

Maybe after he had his GED, he could look for another job. If he found one that paid at least close to what
he got working for Adam, he'd take it. And if Adam hadn't
found someone else by then, and if he hadn't lost interest in
Bo, maybe they could give some of that "boyfriend stuff"
a try.

Until then, as much as it broke him to hurt Adam
and say no to something they both wanted so badly, friendship was all they could have.

Chapter Thirteen

Adam tossed his bag of sweaty workout clothes onto the sidewalk and ran a hand through his shower-damp hair, grateful for the short-lived cooling effects of evaporation. Even in the dead of autumn, afternoon temperatures in Las Vegas sweltered. If Bo weren't so predictable and punctual, he would've taken advantage of the gym's air-conditioning a while longer.

A soft, feminine throat-clearing drew Adam's gaze to a middle-aged woman with gentle brown eyes and skin the same rich mahogany as Kyle's. She scrunched her brow and offered a hesitant smile. "I'm so sorry to bother you, but you wouldn't happen to be the Beast, would you?"

Instinct had Adam hardening his expression, and the woman took a step back. It wasn't until she shifted that he spotted the small boy by her side. He couldn't be more than eight years old. Probably closer to six or seven. The woman tucked the child closer and held up a palm in apology. "I know it must be terrible to have people invade your privacy like this. I'm so sorry. I never would've said anything except Trey and his father are big MMA fans. You're their favorite fighter. He was so excited, and I just... didn't think."

On a normal day, Adam would've let the woman apologize and go on her merry way. He rarely, if ever, chatted with his fans. That was part of the persona. Not one he enjoyed, but one Kyle encouraged. He'd said it would make Adam more elusive and keep his name on the public's lips. People wanted what they couldn't have, after all.

Still, Adam often wished things were different. He yearned for a connection with his supporters. Something more emotionally satisfying than being a lumbering oaf that terrified them, at the very least. Something akin to the relationship his father had with his followers.

Bradford Littrell lived for his fans. He was a legend in the boxing world. A legend that overshadowed Adam's every waking move, as it had since he was a child. There was no such thing as being good enough when his father was the best. Especially not when he chose to go into a "bastardized" version of fighting instead of following in his old man's footsteps.

The woman gave her son's shoulder a squeeze. She murmured another apology and led the little boy away. Adam shook his head to rid it of the heavy, irritating thoughts his father's ever-present influence always brought to mind. His jaw relaxed and a smirk worked up his cheeks when a memory of Bo overtook that moment of darkness. How many times had Bo fussed at him about tabling his outer asshole in favor of being his true self?

"Wait." Adam jogged toward the woman and her young son. They both turned, the mother's brows lifted in surprise even as the boy's face split into a grin. Adam crouched on the ground so he was eye level with the child. "Sorry for being grumpy. I've been studying a lot lately. It makes me kinda cranky sometimes. Are you in school, Trey?"

The little boy's eyes widened to the size of dinner plates. He shot a look at his mother, who gave him an encouraging nod, then returned his big, blinking brown gaze to Adam. "Y-yes, mister. I'm in first grade."

Adam spent the next fifteen minutes chatting with Trey and his mother, Elsa. He urged the boy to study hard, mind his parents, and not beat on his little brother. Then he listened to the kid stumble over his own words as he told Adam about his soccer team, his latest art project, and how his best friend Niles would *never* believe he'd met the Beast.

"Well, how about we give him some proof? Wanna take a selfie with me?"

Trey squealed and tugged at his mother's sleeve. "Momma, can we? Can we, please?"

Elsa beamed with the soft, sweet, tolerant love of a mother as she nodded and removed her cell phone from the front pocket of her purse. They took at least a dozen different photos before Trey was satisfied. Then Adam signed the bill of his ball cap, ruffled his hair, and waved the little family on their way.

Adam shifted to face the entrance of the gym, his gaze catching on a familiar pair of twinkling green irises.

Bo stood several yards away, leaning against the sleek hood of Adam's Maybach. His arms were folded, and a smug grin flashed his pearly whites.

Shaking his head and prepared for a razzing, Adam approached his cocky little friend. "Go ahead, do your worst."

Arching a brow, Bo pushed away from the car. "That was precious and adorable. I'm proud of you." Adam remained silent, waiting for the inevitable zinger, but Bo's smirk slipped into a genuine smile instead. He snatched Adam's gym bag off the sidewalk, grabbed his wrist, and tugged him toward the car. "We now have even more reason to celebrate. We're official GED graduates, plus you made that little boy's entire year. I'd say drinks are in order."

Adam still couldn't believe he'd survived the GED exam. Bo's excitement after receiving their results had been all the reward Adam needed, but Bo deserved something more. Drinks, at the very least. But he'd have to think of something else. Something bigger.

He shook Bo loose at the passenger door and slipped into the driver's side himself. Over the past few months, Bo's anxiety about driving in the heavy Vegas traffic had lessened. Slightly. But whenever he could, Adam preferred to drive, if for no other reason than it allowed Bo to relax.

They decided on the same club that had booted Bo out on his ass six weeks prior. It'd become their standard haunt since then, one Bo allowed him to pay for only because Adam had damn near gotten on his knees and begged. It wasn't until Adam pointed out the elite club provided high-end security—something Bo had grown to respect the importance of after spending over two months by Adam's side—that he'd finally caved. The club's prices were well out of Bo's means, but for the sake of their security, he allowed Adam to foot the bill.

It wasn't like they went out drinking on the regular, anyway. Alcohol wasn't part of Adam's approved diet, and Bo couldn't hold his liquor to save himself.

A truth that became inherently obvious a few short hours later.

"You were so dang cute with that kid today." Bo grinned, big and dopey. His words slurred ever so slightly, and his eyes were glassy behind the glare of his lenses. "I'm not sure you've ever been that stinkin' adorable before. Like, not ever."

Adam chuckled and sipped at the water he'd switched to after his first drink. He was all about celebrating, but getting shitfaced wasn't his MO. Bo, on the other hand, needed exactly one drink to get him sloshed. And tonight he was cutting loose. Three drinks in and the poor guy was a sozzled mess.

"What do you say we head home?" Adam waved at the server for their private VIP lounge and pretended to sign the air, signaling for the check. The woman nodded and disappeared for the bar.

"Home." Bo hummed and closed his eyes. "I like that. I like living in your home. My home. *Our* home."

Damn. Adam straightened his shoulders. That sounded nice, didn't it? *Our home.*

Bo's glazed eyes drifted open and met Adam's with bleary focus. "Would you fire me if I kissed you right now?"

"H'okay." Adam hopped to his feet as a zing of bright hot lust arrowed straight into his groin. "It's definitely time to get you home."

"You wouldn't, would you?" Bo frowned and swayed to a standing position, stumbling as soon as he was upright.

Adam caught him but was careful to keep distance between them. Bo's frown deepened as he took a deliberate step forward. His slender body pressed flush against Adam's, and for a brief pause, Adam allowed himself to press back.

"I'mma kiss you now." Bo snaked his arms around Adam's waist and lifted onto his toes. His soft, plump lips brushed Adam's chin when his senses kicked back into gear at the last moment and he turned his head.

"Bo." Adam gripped Bo's shoulders and eased him away. The painful erection trapped behind the stiff fabric of his designer jeans throbbed in protest, but Adam forced the head with a brain to keep control. "You don't want to do this."

"Don't I?" Bo lifted his brows. "Says who? You gonna fire me if I do? I don't think so. You wouldn't. You're too squishy-hearted."

Adam huffed out a laugh. "Squishy-hearted?"

"Yup." Bo popped the *p* at the end with an exaggerated smack of his lips. "You're a big ol' softy who I wanna get very, very naked."

"Fuck." Adam groaned and held Bo firmly at arm's distance. "You're drunk. We can't do this. I'm going to take you home and put you to bed."

Bo's brows waggled as he struggled to free himself from Adam's grip. "Yes. Bed. Bed's better than a bar for naked stuff."

Have mercy. Adam closed his eyes and willed himself the strength to do what was right.

The server dropped off their check, and Adam had to free Bo to sign. He wrapped around Adam like a vine, the evidence of his drunken arousal pressing against Adam's thigh.

"Kiss me." Bo rocked his hips and clawed at Adam's back. "*Kiss me.*"

Adam carefully extracted himself from Bo's arms and once again held him at bay. "Bo, listen to me. You've had a lot to drink. I don't want you waking up in the morning and regretting this. Let's get you home and put you in *your own bed.*"

Bo's brows furrowed as he yanked himself out of Adam's hold. "I don't care if I'm drunk. I know what I want."

"Okay." Adam drew out the word. He ran a hand through his hair to give himself a moment to think. "You know I want this too. Hell, I've wanted to kiss you since that first day you showed up on my front porch. But there are reasons we've kept our relationship platonic all this time. Rational, realistic reasons. We can't let one night of lowered inhibitions get the better of us."

"Fine." Bo stomped his foot. Literally stomped his damn foot like a five-year-old throwing a temper tantrum. "I'll be good for now. But you better brace yourself, 'cause it won't be coffee I'mma use to wake you in the morning."

With that, Bo turned on his heel and left.

It took Adam a full minute to get his wits about him as images of all the many, many ways he'd dreamt of

Bo waking him danced through his mind. When he finally came back to earth, he cursed under his breath and hurried from the bar. He had a very drunk Bo to get safely home.

Chapter Fourteen

Countless butterflies attacked Bo's queasy, hungover belly with the unforgiving beat of their wings. He groaned and placed a hand over his stomach as memories from the night before ran through his throbbing head in a taunting stream fueled by shame and remorse.

He didn't regret asking Adam to kiss him. Not really. Had he said yes, Bo would've been thrilled to wake naked in his bed rather than tangled in the sheets of his own, fully clothed. But Adam hadn't said yes.

It made sense. Bo couldn't fault Adam for turning down his drunken come-on. After all, hadn't Bo been the one making sure their relationship remained platonic the past few months? Hadn't he been the one pushing Adam away despite the relentless pull that kept trying to draw them together?

Without the brain-numbing power of alcohol twisting his good senses, Bo's stupidity stood out like a shiny beacon of absurdity. Why had he tried to push himself on

Adam? There was no possible positive outcome. Not because Adam didn't want Bo, but after months of being denied, there was no way he'd accept Bo's drunken flirtation as anything other than an error in judgment.

But it wasn't. Not this time. He was tired of fighting his desires and heartsick from watching Adam do the same. And why should they? Bo trusted Adam. He hadn't at the beginning when he hadn't known the man, but he did now. Even if giving in to their physical cravings wound up ruining their relationship, Adam wouldn't screw him over. He wouldn't fire Bo without warning or kick him to the streets, destitute and alone.

At the very least, Adam would give him time to find somewhere else to go. And now that he had his GED, Bo had a better chance of getting another job. Not just a job, but a *good* job. One that might pay a comparable wage.

He rubbed at his temple as he headed for the kitchen. It was Sunday, so despite his inebriated threat, there would be no waking Adam. With coffee or without. This was Adam's only day to sleep in, so Bo wouldn't bother him. But as soon as he got up, they could pick up where they'd left off. Hopefully with Adam's tongue down Bo's throat and a whole heck of a lot less clothing.

When Bo rounded the corner into the living room on a beeline for the kitchen, his bravado drained away with a whimpered yelp. A blistering flush crept up his neck to heat his cheeks as Adam glanced up from his lounge on the couch.

It was barely eight o'clock in the morning. Why was Adam already awake? No, scratch that, *how* was Adam already awake? It took Bo forever to pry him out of bed. He'd never once seen him get up under his own power before 10:00 a.m. at the earliest.

"How are you awake right now?"

Adam rested the book he'd been reading on his chest. He offered a shrug and a small smile. "I set an alarm."

Bo raised his brows in disbelief. "An alarm woke you up? How?"

"By beeping really loud and on repeat." Adam's smile turned wry. "Believe it or not, I've been finding my way outta bed on my own for thirty-eight years before you came into my life."

"But I thought your PAs woke you up." Panic had the warmth in Bo's cheeks cranking up to a simmering scald. Had he been doing something he wasn't supposed to do? Did Adam not want him climbing into bed with him and.... *Crap.*

Adam chuckled and pushed to a sitting position. He slipped a bookmark between the open pages and set his book on the coffee table. "I usually had them pop their head in to make sure I didn't hit snooze too many times, but that's about it. However, when you took it upon yourself to rouse my ass with those adorably frustrated grunts and shakes, I decided it was a much more enjoyable way to wake up."

"You mean...." Bo's jaw dropped. "That wasn't part of the job? Kyle told me you were impossible to wake up. He said I'd have to 'get physical' and asked if I was okay with that. I never would have—"

"Of course he did. Fuckin' bastard." Adam snorted. "Don't worry, I wasn't complaining, was I? I *am* a pain in the ass to wake up, but it's usually my ass feeling the pain, not someone else's. It was a nice change of pace. Plus, it got you into my bed. Even if it was innocent in nature."

Breath rushed from Bo's lungs as his heart thrummed to life at breakneck speed. Adam wanted him as much as he wanted Adam. He couldn't possibly doubt that. So why couldn't he ask for what he wanted now that he was sober?

Adam cleared his throat. "Anyway, I set my alarm because I wasn't sure how early you'd be up and wanted to make sure we cleared the air before things had a chance to get uncomfortable. I don't want you thinking anything's changed. You were drinking and riding high on your GED success. Things were said you didn't mean. That happens to us all, and it didn't bother me in the least. Everything between us is still 100 percent as it was, okay?"

It really wasn't fair how perfect Adam was. He'd gotten up early on his day off to ensure Bo didn't worry about how big of a fool he'd been the night before.

The only problem was, Bo wanted things to change. He didn't want things to be as they were. He was ready for more, even if that more was a gamble. It was a risk worth taking.

"What if I meant what I said?" His voice came out gruff and pitched far lower than normal. "What if I really did want you to kiss me?"

Adam swallowed. The lump at his throat bobbed with the exaggerated movement. He drew a knee up on the couch so he could face Bo more directly. "Did? Or do?"

"Do. Definitely do." A rush of courage bolstered by Adam's low groan spurred Bo to move. He rounded the couch and stopped in front of Adam. Stormy gray irises, darkened by the desire evident in their depths, met his own hungry gaze. "What about you? Did? Or do?"

"Fuck. *Do*. It's always been do." Adam twisted on the couch so his feet were flat on the floor. His strong fingers dug into Bo's hips and dragged him down to straddle his lap. Their cocks grazed through the thin fabric of their pajama pants, and a mingled moan laced the air before Bo crushed his mouth over Adam's.

The lingering mint of Adam's toothpaste tingled Bo's tongue, warring with the bitter bite of his coffee. Rough lips and the burn of beard stubble paired deliciously with the dance of tongues and frantic rush of greedy hands.

Bo couldn't get close enough. Everything in him screamed for more. After so many months of restraint, of shoving back his wants and needs, they came rushing to the surface now with choking intensity. He rocked his pelvis into Adam, relishing the hard heat that pressed back and the strong hands, lips, and tongue that matched his desperation so acutely. He couldn't touch, taste, or feel everything at once, but he tried.

He slid his hands beneath the fabric of Adam's form-fitted T-shirt. At the first touch of skin on skin, a whimper passed his lips. Adam broke their kiss, his hands gripping Bo's hips as they both panted for air.

"If we don't stop now, I'm afraid I'll push too far." Adam's voice was gravelly and strained. "I want this, Bo. Fuck, do I ever want this. But I need to be sure you do too. Why don't we give ourselves some space to breathe and regroup after a shower?"

Bo dug his fingers into Adam's shoulders when he made to shift Bo off his lap. He wasn't going to let Adam push him away. Not now. No frickin' way. "Trust me, I want this. I've wanted it as long as you have. I'm down for a shower, but only if we're getting one together. Either way, shower or no shower, I want you naked. Like, now. I might combust if I don't feel your skin against mine in the next three-point-two seconds."

Adam growled and drew Bo down for another mind-bending kiss. When they pulled apart, minutes could have passed. Or hours. It didn't matter. All that mattered was getting Adam naked and inside him. He couldn't take the wait any longer.

"Please." Bo lowered his forehead to Adam's, their erratic breaths falling into synchronized harmony as Bo rolled his hips in a matching rhythm. "I need you. I want you. Take me to bed. *Please.*"

"I… shit, Bo. I can't. Not now." When Bo halted his movements, his heart plummeting to his stomach, Adam knuckled a finger under his chin. "Hey, look at me. I'm not saying no. I'm saying *not right now.*"

Weren't they the same thing? Bo forced a nod and pulled away. But before he could slide off Adam's lap, Adam wrapped those strong arms around his waist and held him as a willing prisoner against the body he craved but couldn't have.

"I want our first time to be special." Adam rubbed his nose over Bo's. "I don't have the time right now to worship you the way I want. My training camp starts this week, so my Sundays are no longer my own. I've gotta be at the gym in forty-five minutes."

Bo nuzzled into Adam's neck to hide his pout. He was Adam's PA. He should've been the one reminding Adam of his morning obligation, not the other way around. How had he forgotten about the training camp? Too much booze, that's how. And not enough Adam. His eyes fluttered closed when Adam stroked a hand in slow, rhythmic circles over his back.

"I know this is going to sound stupid, but I'm going to miss you." Bo walked his fingers up the back of Adam's neck and toyed with the hair there. "You'll let me drive you, right?"

Adam chuckled, and the deep, resonating tones tingled through Bo's chest. Zaps of electricity fired under his skin as the vibrations traveled outward.

"Why don't you join me? Not to work out, but you haven't been inside my gym yet. You could come see what I do there every day. Meet some of the guys. Maybe watch me kick some of their asses in the practice ring."

Adam wanted to introduce Bo to the men he spent so many hours of his life training with? Bo pushed away so he could meet Adam's gaze. It was far too early to read anything into the request, even though his heart yearned to believe there might be more between them than physical desire.

Still, Adam had never asked Bo to join him at the gym before. It had to mean *something*, right?

Bo grinned, his heart thrilling beneath his ribs when Adam returned the expression with a wide, toothy smirk of his own.

"Okay, but only if you promise I get Naked Adam later."

Laughter barked up Adam's throat. He bucked his hips so their cocks collided and a delicious warmth seeped into the very center of Bo's being.

"You can have all the Naked Adam you can stomach." Adam threaded the fingers of both hands into the hair at Bo's nape. He pulled Bo down for a soft, sweet, gentle kiss. Their tongues met briefly, a promise of what was to come rather than anything meant to encourage their current situation. Then he smacked Bo's butt. "Come on. The sooner we get to the gym, the sooner we can get naked."

Adam didn't need to ask him twice. Bo bounced off his lap, hiding a groan at the sight of Adam fully erect beneath the forgiving fabric of his lounge pants.

In a few short hours, that would be all his. All he had to do was survive watching Adam get all sweaty and hot. No big deal.

Rolling his eyes for his own benefit, Bo hurried to grab a shower. A very, *very* cold shower.

The afternoon couldn't come fast enough.

Chapter Fifteen

Despite it straying from his typical gym uniform, Adam wore compression shorts under a looser-fitting pair. The same look he'd adopted for his evening workouts whenever Bo joined him. It didn't stop him from getting hard-ons, but it kept them somewhat under control. More so than they'd be without the tight fabric in place, at least.

The ride to the gym had been pure torture. He'd driven, which left Bo free to do as he pleased. Something that had never been an issue before but proved a rather large one now that the promise of sex loomed between them. Bo's hands and mouth had tormented Adam with nips, licks, and strokes that damn near undid him.

By the time they'd pulled into the parking lot, Adam was so revved up he almost gave in when Bo begged to wrap those gorgeous lips around his cock and finish him off.

But he'd refused. He'd held his ground. After kissing Bo brainless—an easy feat, considering he'd gotten himself just as worked up—Adam eased him away. One look at Bo's kiss-swollen lips and lust-drunk eyes was all the reminder Adam had needed.

After two fucking months of abstinence and longing, he was going to take his time with Bo. He was going to explore every inch of his skin with his hands, then retrace those steps with his lips and tongue. Bo would be writhing and pleading for release before Adam even considered seeking that welcoming heat and making the man his.

It had taken an excessive amount of time—and a great deal of internal distraction in the form of chanting boring statistics—before Adam could exit the vehicle and enter the gym. And now, with the most strenuous part of his routine out of the way, his distraction level was increasing.

Bo sat on a rickety folding chair in the corner of the gym out of Adam's line of sight. Keeping him at a distance had been necessary after Adam's focus proved iffy when their gazes kept meeting. The sexual tension hung thick and heavy between them, even without the constant eye contact. It served as a relentless diversion from the task at hand.

Not that he'd go back and change his mind about inviting Bo. He'd seemed thrilled by the request, and having him there—while distracting—also proved motivating. Who wanted to look like a weakass pansy in front of the man they hoped to bed? Certainly not him.

Adam slipped through the springy tape-covered ropes of the training ring. His head coach, Eddie Vasquez, waited for him in the corner beside Kyle, who'd shown up a few minutes prior with a shit-eating grin on his face.

"I see Little Bo Peep is in the house." Kyle chortled when Adam slammed a gloved fist into his opposite palm and glared him down. "Still on edge, I see. Haven't gotten laid yet, or did it fail to live up to expectations?"

Adam spit out his mouthguard and charged Kyle, pinning him into the padded corner. "Don't fuckin' talk about him like that."

Eddie placed a hand on Adam's bare chest and shoved. Not enough to make Adam move but enough to get his attention. "Save it for the ring, son."

"I'm already in the damn ring." Adam gave the ropes a shake but stepped clear of Kyle's personal space. "Don't say shit to Bo. If you hurt him, I'll pound your ass into dust."

And he would too. Fuck his manager. He was a few short months away from not needing one, anyway. Maybe. Depending on how training went. Either way, if Kyle even thought about saying something that made Bo uncomfortable, he'd be worm food.

Kyle's eyes glistened with mirth. "You know I'm only fucking with you. I *want* you two to get together. You're a miserably lonely son of a bitch, and he's perfect for you, if you'd open your damn eyes and look. That's why I picked the guy."

Adam cut his gaze to where Bo sat on the edge of his seat. His brows popped over the top of his glasses, and his knuckles blanched under the pressure as he fisted his hands in his lap. He offered a hopeful half smile when he caught Adam looking.

Normally, Adam didn't break character at the gym, and the Beast never smiled. But it was damn near impossible not to grin back, especially when Bo's shoulders relaxed and he beamed in return.

A heavy hand pounded Adam on the back. When he shifted his gaze to glower at Kyle, Kyle guffawed. "Now that's what I'm talking about. I knew that kid would be good for you. He's even got your sour ass *smiling* 'n shit."

Eddie handed Adam his mouthguard and gave Kyle a "get lost" scowl. When Kyle obliged and hopped from the ring, Eddie squeezed Adam's shoulder. "All Kyle's shit aside, I'll admit I've noticed a change in you lately. I'm happy for you, but don't let it get in your way, whatever it is. It's crunch time, son. If you wanna keep your title, you gotta focus. There's no room for distractions, you feel me?"

Across the ring, Adam's sparring partner for the day slipped under the ropes. They exchanged nods before Adam shook Eddie's hand free of his shoulder. He pounded his fists together at the knuckles. "I feel you, coach. Don't worry. I'm focused—110 percent."

Eddie gave a salute and exited the ropes. Adam shifted his attention to the wall of early-twenties muscle bouncing on his toes and jabbing at the air in the opposite corner.

His mentor had it right. He damn well better be focused and on his A game. Not only did he put himself at risk if his concentration wasn't solid during a fight, he also jeopardized his career.

Rather than glancing at Bo to offer a wink of acknowledgment before the fight began, Adam kept his sights on his opponent. They entered the center of the ring, touched gloves, and it was game on.

Bo would get every ounce of Adam's devotion later, but for now, the Beast had work to do.

"I'm *fine*. I swear." Adam swatted at the ice pack Bo kept trying to press against his cheekbone. "I've suffered plenty worse. Hell, you've seen me a hundred times more fucked-up than this. I was fine then, and I'm fine now. Promise."

Bo looked anything but convinced. He bit his lip and bounced on the balls of his feet, clutching at the towel-covered bag of ice with both hands, his eyes glued to the swollen gash beneath Adam's left eye.

It was true. He was fine. Granted, he'd been clocked good, but that wasn't anything new.

Still, the whole ordeal had shaken Bo. He'd appeared on edge before the match even started, but by the time it was over, he was wide-eyed and ashen-faced. During the drive home, he'd sat huddled against the passenger door as if he were terrified to touch Adam. And now? All he wanted to do was shove painkillers down Adam's throat and hold ice over his injuries.

Just fuckin' great. So much for the afternoon of hot, steamy passion he'd had planned. Bo was too worried about mothering Adam to consider taking him to bed.

"How about a bath?" Bo scrunched his brows until they hid behind the thick upper frame of his glasses. "A hot bath might feel good. I can draw you one. I even have a lavender-and-chamomile bath bomb. It'll relax you."

Adam didn't want to relax. He wanted to get Bo naked and…. A thought niggled its way into his brain, and he grinned. "A bath sounds great."

"Yeah?" Bo's eyes lit up. He stopped bouncing and beamed. "Okay. How hot do you want it?"

"I don't take many baths. Make it however hot you like it." Adam accepted the ice when Bo passed it over. He held the freezing pack to his cheek. "I'll keep this here while you do your thing."

"Okay. Yeah. Perfect. I'll come get you when it's ready." Bo scurried toward the stairs, tripped over his feet halfway up, face-planted, then shot Adam a thumbs-up as he clambered upright. "I'm good. Sorry. Be just a minute."

Bo's clumsy eagerness had always been one of Adam's favorite parts about the man. But in that moment, it did something unexpected to his heart. It twisted, thumped, and plummeted to his stomach.

There was little doubt the physical closeness Adam craved from Bo went beyond mere lust. Sure, he was horny as hell for Bo, but that wasn't all there was. Something Adam had never felt toward another brewed beneath the surface, taunting and teasing even as it promised both heartache and wonder.

He wasn't in love with Bo. At least, he didn't think he was. Love wasn't something he was well versed in, yet he was savvy enough to know it didn't happen overnight. Nor did it happen in two months. Especially not when they hadn't even slept together during that time. Love only happened when two people were physical and intimate. It required a commitment. A guy couldn't fall in love with his friend. That's not how it worked.

Right?

Adam scowled as he traipsed up the stairs. He found Bo in his bathroom, crouched by the tub and swirling his hand in the steaming bath. The jets were on, and fizzy bubbles that smelled as Bo promised—of lavender and chamomile—drifted over the surface of the water. Bo turned when Adam's gym shoes squeaked on the tile.

"Oh, I was going to come get you. It's still filling."

"I think it's full enough." Adam set his ice on the counter and yanked his T-shirt over his head. He'd already showered at the gym, but a bath didn't sound half-bad. The soothing aroma was already doing its job. Too bad sleep and relaxation were smack dab at the bottom of his to-do list.

Bo swallowed and jerked to a standing position. His eyes cut to Adam's bare chest, flitted down his belly, and hovered over his crotch. That penetrating gaze was all Adam's dick needed to signal it was time to party. It throbbed, and Bo's teeth slammed together with a snap of his jaw.

Adam hid a grin as he reached around Bo and shut off the water. He made sure to press his body against Bo's and relished the high-pitched whimper that met his ear. Without stepping away, he curled an arm around Bo's waist and held them flush. "There's plenty of room for two."

"Oh God." Bo snaked his arms up Adam's back and placed his hands over his shoulder blades. "Are you sure? That guy hit you hard. If you need—"

Adam tipped Bo's chin and used his lips to halt his protest. Bo opened for him, and their tongues met in a languid dance. He didn't pull back until Bo had melted in his arms. "All I *need* is you."

Chapter Sixteen

o's knees nearly gave out when Adam moved away. He grasped the edge of the granite counter to steady himself and thanked everything good in the world he'd done so when Adam's next move was to drop his shorts. And his underwear. All at once.

"Oh crap." Bo wobbled on trembling legs and redoubled his grip on the counter. He tried to force his eyes upward, but they latched on to Adam's impressive dick and wouldn't let go.

A rumbling laugh filled the room, and Adam waved a hand in front of his groin, snapping Bo out of his cock trance. "I'm hoping the whole bug-eyed thing means you like what you see, but I'm hoping even more you'll return the favor. I want you naked."

Bo curled his lips in as his gaze raked over every perfectly sculpted muscle on Adam's body. How did a man like that want a twig like Bo? The daily workouts had made precious little change to his slender frame.

Heat rose up his chest and bloomed over his face. Under the harsh, bright bathroom lights, there'd be no hiding from Adam. Would he realize his mistake when he got Bo undressed and saw how little he had to work with? The flush boiled hotter as his eyes darted back to Adam's dick. It was at least twice the size of his.

This was a mistake.

"Hey. Look at me." Adam stepped closer, placing his cool palms over Bo's flaming cheeks. Bo did as Adam asked, his pulse racing when their gazes met. "We don't have to do this. It's never too late to say no or stop. I don't want you to feel uncomfortable. Not for even a second."

"Ugh. I *do* want this. More than anything. I just…." Bo glanced between them and frowned. Adam's Greek godlike body was utter perfection no matter what angle he viewed it from. "What if I'm not, you know, *enough*? I don't want to disappoint you."

This was stupid. When had he ever worried about his body? The few men he'd been with had never much cared what he looked like. He'd never had time to really date anyone, so they'd been stupid hookups he always regretted later.

Was that the difference now? Was it because he cared for Adam? Because he gave a crap what Adam thought?

"Bo." Adam grazed his thumbs over Bo's cheekbones. His face was drawn into hard, serious lines. "You will never disappoint me. You're a stunning man, both inside and out. I'm insanely turned on by you and have been since day one. More so now than then, though, and not because your body changed from exercise."

The steam from the bath hung between them like a physical representation of the lust and longing that had colored their relationship from the start. Adam was right. Whatever he'd felt for him that first day, it was nothing compared to how he felt now. It was more than physical attraction that drew him to Adam.

"I'm a man who appreciates beauty, as evidenced by my initial reaction to you." Adam lifted one corner of his lips in a lopsided grin. His thumbs continued to stroke Bo's cheeks. "However, what really gets me is what's inside. And you, Beauregard Wilkins, have a gorgeous heart."

"Cheese and rice." Bo blew out a breath and clamped his hands over Adam's wrists. "You know all the right things to say, don't you?"

Adam chuckled. "I say it how it is, that's all. I'm a no-bullshit kinda guy. I've found sticking to the truth is the best way to get what you want outta life."

He could call it that if he wanted, but Adam wasn't spouting words aimed at getting Bo to cave. Most guys in this situation could probably come up with a suave comment or two to get themselves laid. But that wasn't Adam's goal. He wanted Bo to be comfortable. To feel beautiful, or at the very least believe he was in Adam's eyes. A feat his words had managed to accomplish. For now, at least.

"Okay, so what I'm hearing you say is you want me to strip."

"*Ding, ding, ding.* We have a winner." Adam's grin lit up the room, putting the vanity spotlights to shame. "Bob, why don't you show the man what he's won?"

"Bob?" Bo screwed up his face. "Who's Bob?"

Adam gaped. "Holy shit. Are you so young you don't know who Bob Barker is? The host from *The Price is Right*?"

"Don't you mean Drew Carey?"

Shaking his head, Adam let his hands fall and his shoulders slump. "I really am a dinosaur, aren't I?"

All levity aside, Bo didn't want Adam to fall down the same insecure rabbit hole he'd just clawed free of. Being naked—even with a body as flawless as Adam's—could make a guy feel vulnerable. Especially if he was standing there alone in his bareness.

With unsteady hands, Bo pulled his T-shirt over his

head. He dropped it to the floor and braced himself for Adam to cringe with barely hidden disappointment. But Adam didn't. He straightened his shoulders, his eyes alert and sparkling as he took in Bo's revealed flesh.

A twinge of self-doubt had Bo folding his arms to cover the flatness of his chest. "You may be a dinosaur, but you've got the body of a demigod."

Adam flicked his gaze to meet Bo's. His decidedly nonflat pecs flexed as he clenched and unclenched his fists. A flash of wicked mirth mingled with the lust in his stormy eyes. "Demigod? Why only a *demi*god?"

"Oh, for frick's sake." The man was incorrigible, but his flippant confidence did wonders for Bo's. He laughed and gave his shorts a tug. When they fell to the floor—boxer briefs and all—Adam's stare turned predatory. Bo puffed out his chest, puny though it was, and reveled in the admiration. "Get in the tub, you beast, before the water gets cold."

Rather than slipping into the bubbles as instructed, Adam stalked forward and scooped Bo into his arms. Bo flailed in surprise, then clung to Adam's shoulders as he lowered them both into the sudsy, aromatic water.

Bo waited for Adam to stretch out, and then he shifted to straddle his lap, as he'd done on the couch that morning. He planted his palms on the slick flesh of Adam's pecs to steady himself. Their dicks slid together with such delicious, lubricated friction they both cried out at the contact. Spurred on by the blissful rush of heat and heaven that flooded his body at the feel of Adam's bare skin pressed against his own, Bo rolled his hips again. And again.

"Jesus fuckin' Christ." Adam's fingers dug into Bo's hips. He huffed out a quick breath and rolled his eyes back. "If you do that even one more time, I'm gonna blow my load. You gotta give me a minute here."

It took more restraint than Bo could've imagined to hold still. He yearned to keep moving against Adam, to keep building that delectable coil of tension at his core. His cock pulsed and begged for attention. His skin tingled with the repressed electricity of each firing nerve that cried for more.

But he did as Adam asked. He paused, and he waited. He gave his body time to cool down. To absorb the miraculous feel of skin-on-skin contact he'd craved for two endless months. To enjoy Adam's pinched face and heavy breathing as he battled his own self-control.

After a while, the incessant need to seek relief from his impending orgasm ebbed, replaced instead by an urge to simply find closeness. Adam's countenance had relaxed a touch, so Bo risked movement again. Slowly, carefully, he threaded his arms around Adam's ribs and rested against his chest. He nuzzled into his neck and hummed in contentment when Adam drew his arms around Bo and held him close.

"A bath was a damn fine idea." Adam's words rumbled through his chest and vibrated against Bo's. "But I'm not sure I'll be able to repeat this level of perfection. You might've ruined all future baths for me."

Bo grinned. "It's repeatable. You just have to have the right company."

Adam rested his cheek against Bo's temple and sighed. "I guess that means you're stuck on bath duty for the foreseeable future."

And didn't that sound like its own brand of perfection? Bo's grin widened, but before he could say anything in response, Adam stiffened.

"Shit. Bo, I didn't mean it like that. This isn't part of your job. You have absolutely *no* obligation to—"

Bo shook his head as he pushed to a sitting position. "Don't even go there. Trust me, I'm fully aware that this"—he gestured between them—"has nothing to do with my job. You aren't my boss right now. I don't feel any obligation, nor do I feel any pressure to obey or fear you'll hold anything I do—or don't do—against me. At least, not in a professional sense."

"Not in *any* sense." Adam's lips pressed flat and his brows pinched into a V. "There isn't any pressure here. For any reason."

Adam's concern was unnecessary, but in its own way, also comforting. Not that Bo had doubted Adam's intentions, but it was bolstering to have them confirmed. Truth be told, Bo *was* Adam's employee. It was important to clarify where they both stood. To be sure they were on the same page. Because, if Bo thought this moment was off-the-job but Adam didn't? Or vice versa?

Yeah. That'd be an issue.

"I'm off the clock, Mr. Littrell." Bo winked when Adam cocked a brow. "And yes, no pressure. On either side. You don't have to do anything you don't want to do either."

Adam tipped back his head and howled with laughter. "No worries there, babe. I've wanted to debauch our relationship from the get-go. Just had to wait for you to want the same."

Bo squirmed with delight at the pet name. "Yeah, well, I had to get my head out of my butt first. It's a tight fit up there. Took me a while to pry myself loose."

A growl rolled up Adam's throat and his firm grip returned to Bo's hips. "You really gotta be careful what you say. I was starting to collect myself."

It took Bo a minute to grasp what Adam meant. When the double entendre weaseled its way into his brain, he barked out a laugh. He rocked his hips and smirked. "Hey, I'm not the one who voted for a cool-off period. Me and my tight butt are ready and raring to go when you are."

"*Fuckin' hell.*" Adam gripped Bo's waist and lifted them both out of the water in one swift, seamless move. Water sloshed onto the bathroom floor, and Bo's stomach did a flip as he scrambled to cling to Adam's slippery body.

A slew of colorful curses fell past Adam's lips as he stepped out of the tub and marched into the attached master suite. He dumped Bo onto the bed, still dripping wet and covered in bath bomb remnants, and pointed a finger at his chest. "Don't move."

Grinning, Bo pushed to an elbow so he could enjoy the ridiculous view of Adam's perfect backside as he stalked into the bathroom. A moment later, Adam returned semidry and holding a fresh, fluffy towel. "I'm gonna dry you off so you don't freeze to death. Then I'm gonna explore every inch of your body until you *and* your tight little ass are begging for release." He took a step forward and quirked a brow. "Any questions before we get started?"

"Nope. Not a one." Bo eased off his elbow so he was flat on his back, spreading his arms and legs like a starfish. "I'm all yours, baby."

Chapter Seventeen

Adam took his time drying Bo's glistening, gorgeous body. He'd planned to do so quickly, out of fear he might get cold in the air-conditioning, but the heated glow of Bo's skin told a different story. So Adam lingered over the task. He used the towel some, but mostly he lapped up the water with his tongue. Tasting and teasing. Relishing Bo's mewling whimpers and incessant writhing.

When he reached Bo's flushed cock, he dawdled even further. Licking and kissing and touching everywhere but those places Bo needed it most. By the time he traced his tongue up the seam of Bo's balls for the first time, he was a squirming puddle of incoherent mumbles and clenched fists.

"Holy *crap*." Bo arched his back and clawed at the bedspread when Adam continued down the path he'd started. He trailed his tongue up the underside of Bo's dick, then swallowed him whole. Bo jerked and let out a high-pitched whine. "Ohmygod, ohmygod, ohmygod."

Sucking guys off had never been Adam's cup of tea. It'd also never been anything he'd felt obligated to do. Considering the sum total of his sexual experiences revolved around one-night stands and short affairs with groupies and fans, his responsibilities had been minimal. Most of his partners had simply gotten off on getting the Beast into bed. He hadn't had to do much beyond be present and they were happy as clams.

But it was different with Bo. Adam didn't want to lie back and be a passive participant. He craved him in more ways than a quick fuck could ever satiate. He needed to taste and feel and surround himself in everything that was Bo. Including his delicious cock.

Adam hummed around Bo's dick with a satisfaction he'd never known before. Had he been missing out by not giving head all this time? Or was it this intoxicating and fulfilling only because it was Bo?

When Bo's heavy panting and sensual hip-rolls paired with a low, steady mewling, Adam got his answer. Without a doubt, it was Bo's reactions and the knowledge he drew them from him that made Adam hanker for more. Not that the act itself repulsed him. Anything but, in fact. Bo's dick was the perfect mouthful and his unique flavor the epitome of mouthwatering delight.

Perhaps what they said was true. When you found someone who was your perfect match, everything about them would be too.

"Ya gotta stop." Bo pressed to an elbow and shoved at Adam's shoulder. "Gonna come. Don't wanna. Not yet."

Adam popped his mouth free and smirked when Bo fell back to the bed with a charmingly miserable groan. "I must be doing something wrong. I thought you'd be pleading to come, not begging not to."

Bo lolled his head back and forth. "Nope, nothing wrong. Everything right. Just don't wanna. Not unless you're inside me." He twisted his hips, desperately seeking friction and finding nothing but air. He whimpered and bent his head to meet Adam's gaze. "Please. I need you. Gonna die if I don't have you."

Adam's body tightened as Bo's words washed through him. His cock throbbed against the mattress, imploring him to heed Bo's request without delay. He slipped up Bo's body until their dicks grazed and a shared moan filled the space between them. "There's the begging I was hoping for."

Lacing his hands behind Adam's neck, Bo pulled him down for a kiss. It was hungry and demanding, yet somehow soft and sweet all at once. "I'll beg all day if you want me to, but it might turn ugly if I don't eventually get what I want."

"Oh, no worries there." Adam stretched toward his nightstand drawer and extracted the lube and fresh box of condoms he'd purchased in hopes this day would come. "I won't last much longer. If you hadn't started begging when you did, I would have."

Adam stole another deep, decadent kiss before sitting back on his haunches between Bo's splayed legs. Under Bo's watchful, greedy gaze, he rolled the condom on and squirted lube into the palm of his hand. He smeared half of it over the latex.

Without being asked, Bo spread his legs farther, positioning a hand behind each knee to keep them bent. It placed his ass and dick on perfect display. "Lube me up, but don't waste time with a bunch of prep. Trust me, I'm ready. More than. I want to feel you, now *and* later."

An animalistic snarl cut through the air. Adam bit his lip to halt the obscenities threatening to follow in its wake. He coated two fingers in lube and rubbed them over Bo's opening, his jaw clenching in response to Bo's throaty moan.

Adam slipped one finger past the tight ring of muscle, and Bo's hands dropped from his knees to fist in the sheets. When he worked in a second, Bo's cock jumped on his belly and he ground against Adam's hand, forcing the intrusion deeper.

"'M'kay, yep. Ready." Bo lifted his head and very deliberately licked his lips. "Let's do this thing."

Taking a steadying breath, Adam removed his fingers, wiped them on the discarded towel, then positioned himself over Bo. He pressed his dick against Bo's lubed ass and edged forward until the tip slid inside. He paused, giving Bo a chance to acclimate, then wrapped his arms behind Bo's shoulders so he could whisper into his ear. "Okay?"

"Totally." Bo hummed and swiveled his hips. "Go 'head. Give it to me, baby. *All* of it."

Never one to turn down a direct order—especially not from Bo and *especially* not when he called him baby—Adam eased the rest of the way in. This time, the brief pause was for his own benefit. The delectable pressure and heat nearly undid what little control he had left.

As soon as Adam moved again, Bo scrabbled at his back, murmuring incomprehensible words in a whiny, pleading voice. He wrapped his slender legs around Adam's waist and pulled him in closer. Burying him deeper. Driving him harder and faster.

The threat of orgasm coiled tight and achy at Adam's core. Fearful he'd blow and leave Bo behind, he worked a hand between their bellies and took Bo's weeping cock in his fist. Bo arched his spine and scratched at Adam's back with frantic hands as he drove them both to the edge.

Bo cried out as a flood of molten heat spilled between them. Adam crushed his mouth over Bo's, drinking his whimpers and mewls as his own release tore through him.

Several minutes—or it could've been hours—later, something poked Adam in the ribs. He grunted but didn't move. His breathing was nearing normal again, but his head was still in the clouds. High as fuck with no hope of falling anytime soon.

"Crap on a cracker, Adam." Bo's voice was hoarse and distant. That irritating little poke returned to Adam's side, this time with more force. "You must weigh a thousand pounds after sex. There's gonna be a Bo-sized pit in your bed if you don't get offa me."

"Shit." Adam struggled to his hands so he could support his own weight, his arms shakier than after one of his most grueling upper body workouts. "Sorry. You okay?"

Bo wriggled his shoulders and grinned. "Frickin' perfect, thanks. Especially now that I can breathe."

"Sorry." Adam repeated the apology, his cheeks flooding with heat. He snatched the towel and wiped the evidence of Bo's release off them both, then tossed it onto the floor. Bo grinned like a loon the whole time, his legs still anchored around Adam's hips.

"I'm gonna hit up the bathroom to get rid of the condom. Do you need anything? Some water, maybe?"

Bo shook his head, his lips shifting into a smirk. "Just you. Hurry back, 'kay?"

Chuckling, Adam pried Bo's legs free and hopped off the bed. He padded into the bathroom, cleaned up, then returned to Bo with a warm washcloth in hand. He pointed to Bo's ass, which hadn't moved an inch since he'd left. "Want a wipe-down?"

Stretching his arms over his head, Bo's jaw cracked on a yawn. He nodded and dropped his legs open. Adam climbed onto the bed, kissing the inside of Bo's knee before cleaning him up. He discarded the washcloth on the floor and gave the covers a yank to free them from the side of the bed Bo wasn't sprawled across.

He scooped Bo's limp form into his arms, knee-walked a few feet, and slid them both beneath the cool sheets. Bo shifted, but only enough so his body pressed flush to Adam's, their legs tangled and his head resting on Adam's shoulder.

"Can we do that again?" Bo's words were slurred

with lethargy, but he tightened his grip around Adam's middle for emphasis. "Like, every day?"

Adam brushed a kiss along Bo's hairline and traced his fingers in soft, concentric circles over his shoulder. "I'm yours for the taking whenever you want me."

"Mmm, good." Bo purred under Adam's touch. "Although, you might regret that open-ended offer when I come in here and wake you up three times a night."

Adam choked back a laugh. Was that supposed to be a threat? He'd slept poorly for months thanks to the man he now held in his arms, struggling to fall asleep and waking frequently from erotic dreams that paled in comparison to the experience they'd shared. "Yeah, that's not happening, babe."

Bo lifted his head and blinked at Adam with heavy lids. "Say what now?"

"You're not going to come into my room in the middle of the night. You might *come* in here, but you aren't coming *in*. If you catch my drift." Adam pressed his lips together to halt his looming grin. When Bo continued to stare at him with exaggerated blinks, Adam huffed out a laugh. "You can wake me up as many times as you want, but if I have any say in the matter, you'll already be naked and in my bed. No need to do anything more than push that sexy body against mine and I'll be ready to go."

"You want me to stay in your bed? Overnight?" Bo tilted his head and frowned. "You don't do that."

Adam pressed his thumb between Bo's brows to smooth the little V that had formed. Bo had a point. Adam didn't do the overnight thing. Nor did he have sex at home. Bo was the first man he'd ever been with in his own bed. The first man he'd ever *wanted* in his bed. And now? He didn't want him to leave it. Ever. "You're right. I *didn't* do that. But I do now. Or at least I want to. With you."

Bo's eyes danced with delight as he nibbled on his upper lip. The corners of his mouth tugged into a smile.

"Yeah?"

"Oh yeah." Adam cupped the back of Bo's neck, guiding him down for a kiss.

"Well, then, good." Bo scrunched his nose before resting his head on Adam's shoulder and snuggling back into his arms. "I wasn't looking forward to making that trek down the hall in my birthday suit. It's a bit nippy in here when you're nekkid."

"Don't worry. I'll keep you warm." Adam rolled on his side and tucked Bo close. "Probably too warm, 'cause I don't plan to let you go."

And he meant that. For better or worse. Hopefully Bo didn't need personal space to sleep, because Adam wasn't giving him any.

Bo peppered kisses over Adam's collarbone and sighed. "That won't be a problem. I've spent two months wishing for this. It's exactly what I want."

"You too, eh?" Adam chuckled. "Good. We can be clingy, codependent assholes together."

Chapter Eighteen

Lulu's self-assigned ringtone—an obnoxious children's song that drove Bo up a wall—echoed through his half-comatose brain. He groaned and burrowed deeper into Adam's warmth. His sister would call back if it was important. Or leave a message. He didn't want to move.

It had been a week since he and Adam first slept together, but they'd done it countless times since. Before bed. In the middle of the night. Before Adam went to the gym. After he got home. It didn't matter what time of day it was, they couldn't get enough of each other.

He still couldn't believe it was happening. Every time he woke up naked beside Adam, he'd have to pinch himself to be sure he wasn't dreaming. And it wasn't only the sex either. Everything about their relationship had changed. Even when Bo was technically "on the clock," he and Adam ignored that fact. There were no more boss and employee moments. Everything was just *them*. Together. Being happy.

Barney the purple dinosaur's overly cheerful sing-song voice cut through the silence again, warbling joyfully about how he loves you, you love him, and everyone's a great big happy family.

Alarm sliced through Bo's groggy mind. He sat bolt upright, panic sending his pulse rate spiking as he fought to free himself from Adam and the blankets. He scrambled across the bed and snatched his phone off the nightstand, then slid the green answer button across the screen and dragged the phone to his ear. "Lu? You okay?"

"There you are." Lulu's irritated voice assaulted Bo's ear. He could hear the pout in it. "Why didn't you answer when I called the first time? What if I'd been dying?"

Bo rubbed a hand over his tired eyes. "I was asleep, Tallulah."

"Oh, bustin' out the real name. What'd I do this time? Breathe wrong?"

Sighing, Bo glanced at Adam, who hadn't budged an inch in his slumber, and scooted back to lean against the headboard. He tugged the covers over his bare lap and willed patience into his sleepy brain. He noted the time before responding. "It's barely six in the morning. What led you to think I'd be awake?"

Lulu huffed in exasperation. "You used to get up by four every day, so sue me for not realizing your schedule changed. Jeez, what am I, a mentalist? Supposed to read your mind or some shit?"

"*Language*, Lulu. What the heck, girl?" Bo held the phone away from his ear briefly to verify it really was his baby sister on the other end. He didn't kid himself that Lulu never cursed, but she was always careful not to do so in his presence. She'd always been a bit of a smart aleck, but considering it was only 6:00 a.m., she was being something extra special this morning. "Is something wrong? You don't sound quite like yourself."

"I'm calling you at the ass crack of dawn. Of course something's wrong."

"Okay." He drew out the word, letting her latest foul language transgression slide in favor of responding to her grumpy admission. "Talk to me. What's up?"

She harrumphed, and he imagined her crossing her arms and scowling in that angsty teenage way she was so skilled at. "I don't like it here. I wanna come home."

He scratched a thumb over his brow and frowned. "What don't you like about it?"

"I don't fit in here. I'm not like these people." Her voice got small, and she sniffled into the phone. "Can I come home? Please? Just for a weekend? I miss you."

Bo scraped his teeth over his bottom lip as he tried to calculate the logistics of getting Lulu to Vegas for a visit. He'd given her his car when she went away to school, so she could drive herself home. But he didn't have a home for her to come back to anymore. He'd need to rent a hotel. And get some time off, something he hoped Adam wouldn't mind giving him.

"Bo?"

"I'm here. Sorry, trying to wake my brain up. Of course you can come visit. How about this weekend? I'll talk to my boss about getting some vacation time."

Lulu was silent a moment before huffing out a breath. "Okay. I've gotta get ready for class now, but can I come Friday night? I could leave right after my last lecture."

"That sounds perfect." Bo schooled his voice to sound enthusiastic. "Call me if you need to talk or anything before then, okay?"

Lulu agreed, and they hung up after exchanging I-love-yous and the standard promises to behave, study hard, and drive safe on the trip home Friday.

Bo let his head fall back against the headboard. "Crap."

"Everything okay, babe?"

Adam's unexpected, gravelly voiced question startled Bo. He yelped, then let out a self-deprecating snigger.

"Jeez, you scared the heck out of me. What are you doing awake?"

"You sounded worried." Adam lifted the covers, revealing his bare, perfectly muscled torso, and opened his arms in invitation.

Bo slipped into the welcoming warmth of his embrace. He allowed the rhythmic circles Adam rubbed over his back to ease the tension Lulu's call had brought to the surface.

"You wanna talk about it?" Adam brushed his lips over Bo's hair when he spoke, leaving a kiss on the crown of his head to punctuate the question. To let Bo know he was there, as he always was.

"Lulu's struggling at school. She wants to come home for the weekend because she misses her dear old brother." Bo walked his fingers up Adam's bicep to buy himself a little time to build his courage. Nerves had his stomach turning. Would Adam be upset with him for requesting time off so last-minute? "Would it, ah, be okay if I took the weekend off? I know it doesn't give you much notice, but I—"

"Babe." Adam stopped tracing patterns over Bo's back and knuckled under his chin. Their eyes met, and Adam smiled. "Of course you can have the weekend off. I'd give you the rest of your life off if I thought you'd be open to the title of Kept Man."

Bo drew back his chin and shook his head in horror. A kept man? As in, what, Adam wanted to foot all his bills so he could laze around and do nothing? Not happening. Not only would he go crazy without something to keep his mind active, but there was no way he'd risk Lulu's future. What if Adam got tired of him? Or started to resent him for loafing off his dollar? He'd be hunting for a job with an unexplained gap in employment. It was hard enough to find work with a proven track record. No one would hire him if he'd fallen off the grid.

Adam chuckled. "I know, I know. You're far too

strong-willed and independent for that, which I respect the shit out of. But the point is, you can have time off whenever you want it. All you gotta do is let me know and it's yours. Just so I don't worry about you when you aren't up my ass in that way I love so much."

Bo rolled his eyes but grinned as he pinched Adam's most ticklish spot—the side of his ribs beneath his armpit. Adam howled and rolled them both until he straddled Bo's lap. He pinned Bo's arms to the bed and pouted. "What was that for? I thought I was being nice."

Nice was an understatement. How many bosses gave their employees unlimited vacation time? And without any real notice. It never ceased to amaze Bo how sweet and wonderful Adam could be. It baffled him to remember how he'd dreaded the idea of working for a man like Adam, yet the perception he'd had couldn't have been any further from the truth.

"Oh, you were." Bo cocked his head and smirked. He bounced his hips so their dicks collided. "I wanted you on top of me, that's all. We've got lots of time to make up for if I'm going to be gone all weekend."

"Whoa, pump the brakes. Who said anything about you being gone all weekend?" Adam scowled. "I thought Lulu was coming here."

The nerves kicked back into gear. Adam had agreed to let him take a vacation, but he'd clearly assumed Bo would be staying around the house. Which would mean he'd still be available in an emergency. Would he change his mind if he knew Bo planned to go to a hotel with Lulu instead of making her stay alone?

"She is. I mean, she's coming to *Vegas*, but I'm going to rent a hotel." Bo cringed when Adam's scowl deepened. "For us both."

Folding his arms over his sculpted chest, Adam squinted an eye. "Why?"

Because Lulu sounded desperate, that's why. No

way was he going to make her stay alone in a hotel when she seemed so down. "She's coming all this way. I want to spend as much time with her as I can."

"Well, yeah." Adam cocked his head. "But I don't get why you'd be able to spend any more time with her at a hotel than you could here. Are you afraid I'll interfere? I'd be happy to ghost for the weekend. As long as I get to come home at night and share a bed with you, I can make anything work."

Adam thought Bo was bringing Lulu into his home? No frickin' way. That was wrong on so many levels. "Ah, I wasn't implying Lulu would stay at your house, baby. I'd never do that to you. She'll be at the hotel, which is why I want to be there. To be close to her."

"Oh, for fuck's sake, Bo." Adam laughed, unfolding his arms so he could pull Bo into them. "You are *not* staying at a hotel. Neither of you are. This is your home. If Lulu is coming to visit, she should stay here, *in your home*. There are four guest bedrooms. There's more than enough space."

A thousand butterflies took flight in Bo's chest. Adam considered his house to be Bo's home? That was…. Bo shivered. That was the best thing ever.

Adam dropped a kiss to the tip of Bo's nose and smirked. "Plus, I'm a selfish bastard. There's no way in hell I'm giving up even a single night with you. Lulu's a big girl, and you said yourself she knows you're gay and sexually active. I'm fine with wearing clothes to bed and abstaining from sex while she's in the house. But there's no reason you can't crawl into our bed and sleep in my arms because Lulu's here."

Our bed? Bo's belly did a flip, and a kaleidoscope of butterflies moved to fill its churning depths. Okay, so maybe he'd spoken too soon. *Our bed* might trump *home*. Maybe. Possibly. He couldn't decide which was better, and at that moment, he didn't much care.

Chapter Nineteen

Adam threw his legs over the side of the bed and scowled into the darkness. Considering he'd spent thirty-eight years sleeping alone—at least twenty of those actively keeping others away—his restlessness made no sense. He should be able to sleep unaccompanied in his own damn bed without issue.

But that clearly wasn't happening. Not without Bo.

In the two weeks since they'd finally given in to their mutual desire, Adam hadn't slept alone once. Bo had shared his bed every night, naked and warm. If Adam had slept like the dead before, he didn't know what to call his sleep with Bo tucked close, their bodies sated and hearts full. He damn near went comatose.

Now, with Bo back in his own room two doors down, Adam was twitchy and on edge. With Lulu in town, Bo had decided they needed to maintain some semblance of propriety and sleep in separate rooms, but Adam's bed had never felt so empty, nor his heart so achy. He missed Bo.

Painfully so.

It was stupid. Bo would only be gone for a few nights, and then all would return to normal. Their *new* normal. The perfection of the past two weeks. Or so he hoped. But there was no guarantee, was there?

That's where the tightness in his chest came from. The fear of the future. All good things had a finite ending, after all. As his career would eventually wind to a close, so too would his relationship with Bo. It was simply a matter of time.

Adam pressed to his feet. He couldn't wallow in bed all night. If he wasn't going to sleep, he should do something productive. Maybe if he busted his ass in the gym, he'd forget for a few minutes how lonely he was and pass out from exhaustion.

After garbing for a workout, Adam crept down the hall. He placed a palm over Bo's door, stealing a moment of comfort from his closeness before tiptoeing down the stairs.

The bright beacon of the kitchen light drew his attention. He frowned. He'd been the last to bed and had shut off all the lights before heading upstairs. As promised, he'd avoided the house until after eleven to give Bo and his sister some time alone. Neither of them had been awake when he'd gotten home, a truth that only fed his insecurities.

Bo hadn't even stayed up for a stealthy good-night kiss.

But maybe he was struggling to sleep too? Maybe they could sneak that kiss now?

When Adam stepped into the kitchen, any hope he'd allowed at the prospect of seeing Bo vanished. In its place, confusion took root.

A tiny sprite of a girl with jet-black hair and pale porcelain skin—a spitting female image of her brother—sat at the breakfast bar. Her hand was wrapped around the neck of a beer bottle, and fat tears spilled down her face. They ran in rivulets over her cheeks, staining them with the remnants of what might've once been dark smoky eye makeup. Now it was a fucked-up mess.

Adam wasn't used to being around females. His world had always been filled with tough men who harbored tough expectations, starting with his father and carrying through with Eddie, Kyle, and the myriad of other men he associated with during training and fights.

Out of both habit and nerves, Adam slipped into Beast mode. Whenever he didn't know how to act, it was always easiest to pretend, so he glowered and crossed his arms. "I thought you were only eighteen. Why are you drinking my beer?"

Lulu let out a squeak of surprise. She jerked, and the beer toppled. Its contents splashed over the counter and formed a puddle near Adam's feet. She blinked up at him, the vivid blue pools—unaided by glasses—the first real noticeable difference between her and Bo. Even her hair was styled in a pixie cut that, from a distance, resembled Bo's artfully disheveled locks.

When she hiccupped and a fresh wave of tears misted her eyes, Adam sighed. He unfolded his arms and grabbed a few towels. Lulu accepted the one he handed her but made no move to sop up the mess on the counter, even when he crouched to dry the floor. He straightened and cocked his head, taking a closer look at the glassiness of her eyes. They might be blue—not green—but he'd seen another Wilkins with that bleary-eyed stare more than once before. "Are you drunk?"

"No." Lulu scrunched her nose in a sneer. "I'm just buzzed."

"Right, and at eighteen, neither is allowed." Adam snatched the dry towel out of Lulu's lax grip and finished cleaning the spill. "Mind telling me why you're awake in the middle of the night, stealing my booze?"

"None of your business, dickhead." She pushed off the stool, stomped to the refrigerator, and pulled out a fresh beer. Popping the bottle's cap with an expertise Adam hadn't gained until at least twenty-five, she took a long swallow before sticking out her tongue. "I can do whatever I want. You aren't in charge of me."

Adam knew nothing about women, and even less about teenagers. He hadn't been around one of those hormonal creatures since he was one himself, but he could vaguely remember spouting off idiotic and rebellious taunts with no real recollection as to why he'd done so or what would've made him stop.

Perhaps being an asshole wasn't the best way to handle the situation. It would give Lulu added reasons to be a brat and to return his snark with more of her own. He held up his hands in surrender. "You're right. You're an adult, and I don't even pretend to be the authoritative parenting type. I'm more about taking orders than giving them."

"*Sure* you are. I can totally see the big, bad Beast taking orders." Lulu snorted, and beer surged out her nose. Her eyes widened, and she dropped her bottle. Again. This time it shattered and covered the kitchen floor in a flood of amber liquid and glass. She squawked, held her nose with one hand, and flapped her free arm. "It burns. Ohmygod, it *burns*."

"Shit." Adam strode across the sea of alcohol—thankful he had sneakers on, since he'd dressed for the gym—and lifted Lulu off the floor. He threw her over his shoulder and carried her flailing, squealing ass into the living room, where he released her on the nearest soft surface.

"You creep." She scrambled to her feet and punched a tiny fist into his stomach. "Wait until I tell my brother what you did. He'll kick your ass."

"Tallulah, what the heck is going on down here?" Bo's groggy voice preceded him down the stairs. He rubbed at his eyes before slipping on his glasses and stopping short two steps from the bottom.

Undoubtedly, Adam and Lulu made quite a sight.

She was poised to aim another punch at his midriff, and he was grinning like it was Christmas morning. Not only did Bo's presence mean he could take the mini hormone monster off Adam's hands, it also meant there was still a chance for that good-night kiss.

"This jackass grabbed me." Lulu pointed an accusatory finger at Adam's chest. "*He grabbed me.*"

Adam took a step back, holding up both hands palms out. "Hey, I was trying to save you from the glass. That's all."

Bo glanced from Lulu's squinty-eyed glare to Adam. He heaved out a purse-lipped breath and rubbed at his temple. "What glass?"

"Does it matter?" Lulu interjected before Adam had a chance to respond. Panic laced her words, and she bounced on the balls of her feet. "He *grabbed* me, Bo. Kick his sorry ass into pulp."

A chuckle fell from Bo's lips. "Have you seen the man? He pummels men three times my size for a living. Even if I wanted to—which I don't—I'd be the one turning into pulp."

"Fine. *Fine.* Whatever." Lulu folded her arms and sulked in that overly dramatic way only a teenager could pull off. "I'm going to bed."

Bo held out an arm to stop her before she could pass him. "I think not." He popped a brow and pointed to the couch. "Sit. You're not going anywhere until I know what really happened. And don't try any of that 'he grabbed me' crap again. I want the truth."

"That *is* the truth." Lulu flounced back to the couch and fell onto it with enough force to send it squeaking over the hardwood floor. "Why is everyone out to get me? Isn't *anyone* on my side?"

Adam didn't envy Bo one second of this drama, but his heart twisted nonetheless. There was something very real and very painful about the words Lulu spoke. He angled his gaze to Bo, whose attention was zeroed in on his sister. The worry was clear in the pinch of his brow.

"I'm gonna go clean up the kitchen." Adam backed in that direction, his belly doing a flip when Bo's eyes met his. The *thank-you* was evident in his nod and that small, sweet smile.

Adam was putting away the mop when Bo trudged into the kitchen twenty minutes later. His shoulders sagged, and he ran a hand through his sleep-tousled waves. "I'm so sorry about that. I don't know what her problem is. She didn't used to be such a handful. She's a really great kid. I swear."

"Independence does strange things to people. Don't take it personally. She'll grow out of it." Adam tossed the beer-soaked rags into the sink. "Did you get things smoothed over?"

Bo scoffed and scrubbed at his face with both hands, shoving his glasses into his hair. "She admitted to the beer. Apparently my straitlaced brainiac of a kid sister is getting drunk on the reg. Swell, huh?"

Neither Bo nor Adam had college days to look back on and compare notes. But Lulu's experience seemed pretty run-of-the-mill to Adam. Wasn't that what kids did? Go off to college, spread their wings, and do superstupid shit?

"Is she doing okay in school?" Adam leaned a hip against the counter and stuffed his fists under his armpits. He had to, or else he'd reach out for Bo. He wanted to feel his solid warmth more than anything else, but he'd never flout Bo's needs to meet his own.

Bo shrugged. "She was vague about it. I have no clue what's going on in that girl's head."

When Bo didn't say anything further, Adam cleared his throat. "I want to be sure you know I didn't touch Lulu inappropriately—"

"Oh God, Adam. No. *No.*" Bo shook his head, his eyes widening beneath his glasses. "I know. I do. I promise.

I never for even a second thought you would have. She's being a giant pain right now. I don't know what possessed her to insinuate such a thing."

"I took her by surprise. That was my fault. Should've told her I was going to grab her, but I acted quicker than I could think. I didn't want her to cut herself on the glass." Adam buried his fists deeper under his arms. "I'm not exactly great with females."

Bo's face softened into a sleepy smile, his lids drooping. "It's late. Why were you awake in the first place? And fully dressed, no less?"

Rubbing a hand over the back of his neck, Adam fought the heat creeping up his cheeks. "Ah, I couldn't sleep. Thought I'd get a workout in."

"You wear me out." Bo chuckled. He took a wobbly step forward and fell—blessedly—into Adam's arms, nuzzling into his chest. "I miss you. My bed's big and lonely."

"*Fuck*. Me too, babe." Adam held Bo close, dropping a kiss to the crown of his head. "One and a half more nights, then we can spend an entire day in bed. To hell with the training camp. I'll let you work me out instead."

Bo nodded against Adam's chest. "Sold. But you have to come out with Lulu and me tomorrow." He peeked up at Adam and grinned. "I might've let it slip you're gay when she wouldn't give up her story. It took one glance at my face for her to guess we're sleeping together. That flipped her switch. All she could talk about after that was you. And us. She asked me about a hundred questions, and the only way I could get her to go to bed was by promising to let her apologize over dinner tomorrow. She wants to get to know you. If that's okay."

Adam beamed, his cheeks cramping under the strain. As far as he was concerned, it was more than okay. "Does that mean I'm allowed to steal a kiss right now?"

"I'll do you one better and say, not only can you steal all the kisses you want, but Lu yelled at me for treating her like a child by sleeping in separate bedrooms."

Adam scooped an arm under Bo's knees, swept him against his chest, and headed for the stairs. "Thank fuck. I'm not sure I could've survived two nights without sleep during a training camp. I'll be sure to thank the little monster in the morning."

Chapter Twenty

Bo let his head fall against the seat back behind him. He grinned at the ceiling, cringing as the two idiots in the front seat hit another off-key note.

What were the chances his baby sister would have a voice as terrible as—if not more so than—Adam's? It was no wonder he'd never heard her sing before now. She probably broke a few mirrors or shattered a water glass or two as a child and decided to avoid it for the sake of their family's finances.

Because, *holy cow*, those two were a special kind of terrible. And together? They might legitimately damage his eardrums. "Could you two take it down a notch? I'd prefer not to get a brain bleed at twenty-five."

Lulu spun around in the passenger seat. A comical grin spread her cheeks, and she bounced her head back and forth to the rhythm of the music. "The night is young, big brother. There's more where this came from. Consider yourself blessed to be surrounded by such talent and skill. It isn't every guy who has a sister *and* a boyfriend who can sing like angels."

Adam offered Lulu a high five and winked at Bo from the rearview mirror. He cranked the volume on his satellite radio, and the caterwauling continued, unhindered by Bo's request for reprieve.

Which, for the first time all night, didn't matter. Bo was no longer paying attention to the tone-deaf wailing. He'd latched on to a single word in Lulu's assertion and couldn't get his brain to let it go.

Boyfriend? Adam Littrell was *not* his boyfriend. Boss, yes. Friend, for sure. Friend with *really awesome benefits*, no doubt. But boyfriend? Not happening. Did Bo dream of such a thing? Yes, every night, but that wasn't in the cards. Adam didn't do romantic, long-term relationships. He'd tire of Bo eventually, and when that happened, they'd either slip back into their boss-employee relationship or Bo would be scrambling to find a new job.

That didn't terrify the ever-loving daylights out of him because things were so perfect right now. No way Adam would tire of what they had anytime soon. Not when the sex was as good as it was. And even though they hadn't done more than curl up together, fully clothed, he'd seemed genuinely pleased to get Bo back into his bed the night before.

By the time they pulled into the garage, Bo was back to covering his ears and griping at every pause in the tuneless warbling drifting from the front seat. Neither Lulu nor Adam seemed to care, as they both decided it'd be a grand idea to bust out *Rock Band* on Adam's Xbox as soon as they entered the house.

Even though only one of them could control the microphone portion of the game, they continued to croon the songs together, taking turns pounding on the drums or strumming the guitar as they did. They tried to get Bo to participate, but he accepted his musical inabilities and chose not to curse those around him with his own faults. Unlike his beloved sister and boss.

The night eventually wound down, and they stretched out on the couch to watch *Saturday Night Live*. Bo drifted to sleep and startled awake as the show wrapped up. He'd somehow migrated from the middle cushion to practically lying on top of Adam. He gave himself a moment to enjoy the warmth of Adam's embrace before pulling free.

At the other end of the couch, Lulu smirked in his direction. "Okay, kids, it's time for bed." She made an exaggerated show of stretching and yawning. "Bo, will you tuck me in? For old time's sake?"

When she fluttered her lashes at him, Bo laughed. "Brush your teeth. I'll be up in a minute."

Lulu hopped to her feet and stopped in front of Adam. She held out a fist and grinned when he pounded it with his own. "G'night, you grumpy bastard. Thanks for hanging. You're loads more fun than my lame-o brother."

"Sweet dreams, mini monster." Adam returned her smile and pulled Bo back into his arms. "You're welcome here anytime."

She shoved a finger down her throat, made a gagging noise, then winked. "Get a room, you guys. You're tainting my innocence."

"Innocence, my ass." Adam chortled and pointed up the stairs. "Brush your teeth. I want a minute with your brother. Unless you want to stick around and watch me shove my tongue down his—"

"Ohmygod. Don't you dare." Lulu covered her ears and squeezed her eyes shut. "I'm going. *I'm going.* No kissy noises until I'm safe in my room with the door shut."

She bolted up the stairs, and Adam turned to Bo with a self-satisfied grin squinting his eyes. "I like her. She's a pain in my ass, but overall, she's a pretty cool cat."

A warmth that had no right to exist wrapped itself around Bo's heart. Adam liked his kid sister, and she clearly liked him in return. It shouldn't matter, but it did. It really, really did. He shifted so he could snake his arms around Adam's ribs. "Is it okay if I join you again tonight?"

Adam narrowed one eye and popped the opposite brow. "Why is that a question?"

"Because with Lulu here, we can't, you know, *do* anything." As ridiculous as it was, Bo's cheeks heated. "I wanted to make sure you wouldn't rather have your bed—"

"*Our* bed, and no, I absolutely would *not* rather have it to myself, if that's what you were gonna say." Adam pulled Bo the rest of the way into his lap and threaded his fingers along the back of his neck. He tipped his chin and brought their lips together for a soft, chaste kiss. "I don't need sex to sleep, but I do need you."

Ten minutes—and lots of decidedly unchaste kiss-es—later, Bo entered Lulu's room in a dopey half daze. She was already in bed, propped against the headboard and thumbing through the glossy pages of a fashion magazine.

Pursing her lips, Lulu set the magazine on her lap and tilted her head. "You've got some stubble burn there, bro. Glad I exited stage left when I did. From the looks of it, he tried to suck your whole face off."

Bo rolled his eyes and leaned a hip on the edge of Lulu's bed. "Bite me."

"I think Adam did enough of that for the both of us." She snorted, then immediately sobered. Her brows drew to-gether, and her lips turned down. "Is he treating you right?"

Leave it to Lulu to worry about him when she had her own stuff weighing her down. He might've been the one who took on faux parent status, but she'd mothered him nearly as much as he'd fathered her over the years. "Seri-ously, Lu?" Bo chuckled and gave her knee a squeeze. "I'm a big boy. I can take care of myself."

Her brows crinkled further. "I don't like that answer. Is he taking advantage of you? Using his boss status to make you do things you don't want? I thought he was making you happy, but if he—"

"He *is*, girl. Relax." Bo shook his head and grinned. "Adam's a good guy. There are no power-dynamic issues. I promise. Everything we do is because we both want to. End of story."

She worked her jaw back and forth. "Do you love him?"

"Okay, that's *so* none of your business." Bo closed his eyes and blew out a breath. Lulu never shied away from the tough questions, nor did she excel at keeping her nose out of places it didn't belong. "Adam and I don't have that kind of relationship. It isn't romantic. We're friends, having a little fun."

"I call bullshit." Lulu folded her arms and smirked. "That ginormous brick wall of a man goes positively gooey at the center when he looks at you. It's nauseating, really, but because you deserve to find some frickin' happiness for *yourself* for once in your life, I'm willing to keep antivomit meds on hand when I visit."

Bo glanced over his shoulder to be sure Adam wasn't lurking in the hallway listening to Lulu's lunacy. When he turned back, her smirk had grown. He narrowed his eyes and ran his tongue along the back of his teeth. "You're imagining things. He's my *boss*, Lu. We're keeping things casual."

"Sure, *casual*, right." Lulu's eyes disappeared into the back of her head. "Adam looks at you like you're Thanksgiving dinner and Christmas morning all wrapped into one, but that's nothing on how you look at him. I know you better, so maybe it's easier to catch your tells, but for real, yo… it's love. With a big ol' capital *L*. And you've both got it. *Bad*."

Bo didn't love Adam. Absolutely *no way* would he be that stupid. He cared for him, as a person, as a friend, and as a boss, but no more. Why would he put his heart on a guaranteed path to destruction? It was bad enough he risked the stability of his and Lulu's financial future for a few selfish moments of ephemeral joy. He couldn't endanger his emotional sanity as well. What good would he be for his sister if he was penniless *and* heartbroken?

"Go to sleep, Lu." He bent over and kissed her forehead. "Dream sweet dreams, and tomorrow? We'll talk. Not about me, and not about Adam, but about *you*. You're not going back to Cali until I know you're okay."

"What, you gonna hold me hostage?" She curled her lip, but her eyes shone with sisterly love. "I don't think ol' Mr. Boss Man would be too pleased with that idea."

Bo stood and ruffled her hair. "Your happiness comes before anything else, Lu. I'm here for you, no matter what that means. I can always find another job, but I've only got one little sister."

"Thank you for letting me visit." Lulu tossed her magazine on the nightstand and slid under the covers. "It's been just what the doctor ordered."

He stopped at the door, his hand resting on the knob, and smiled. "I love you, kid. Sleep tight, and don't let the bedbugs bite."

Lulu groaned at his use of their father's favorite bedtime saying. It was a tradition Bo had carried on after his death. Every single night, he'd tuck her in, kiss her brow, and swear away the bed-sharing creepy-crawlies. She liked to pretend she was too old for the childhood phrase, but the grin accompanying her moans told a different story.

"I love you too, Bo." She yawned and closed her eyes. "Now turn off the lights and get your butt to bed. I betcha there's a gooey-centered Beast already there, waiting impatiently to give you more scruff-burn. Don't keep the poor man waiting any longer than you already have. He might implode."

Chapter Twenty-One

66The room's ready." Adam slid an arm around Bo's slim shoulders and dropped a kiss to his brow. "Do you want to leave our stuff with the concierge and have them deliver it, or should we drop it off ourselves and check out our digs for the night?"

Bo wiggled against Adam's side, beaming up at him with a twinkle in his eye. "If we go to an empty hotel room now, we'll never make it to dinner."

Adam guffawed and drew Bo closer. He sealed their lips for a far-too-brief kiss, ever cognizant of their public locale. Bo had a point. The past month had flown by in a blur of heavy-hitting exercise, comatose sleep, and Bo. Even with all the extra energy he burned during his intense training camp workouts, he was never at a loss when it came time to get his man naked.

And that's exactly what he was, even if Bo didn't want to call it that. Adam had broached the "boyfriend" subject a few weeks prior and been shot down. Nicely, and with amazing conciliatory sex afterward, but shot down nonetheless. Hell, he would've been happy wrangling *any* sort of commitment out of Bo, but he'd held strong.

Bo insisted they couldn't date while he worked for Adam. When Adam made the mistake of suggesting he didn't *need* to work, Bo came up with a hundred reasons why he *did*. Which Adam respected. Bo didn't want to risk his and Lulu's financial freedom on something as unreliable as a romantic relationship. Instead, he aimed to keep Adam at a distance and assure their relationship remained at least somewhat professional.

Unfortunately, Adam's heart was less inclined to follow such a prudent path. He couldn't pinpoint exactly when, but at some point, he'd fallen in love. Hard. And how could he not? Bo was everything he'd never known he needed and more. The thought of losing him terrified Adam. Far more than the idea of losing his upcoming title defense.

Retirement used to be the only thing that could scare the Beast. Now he quivered in his boots thinking about an empty bed. Not because Bo was the best lay he'd ever had—which he was, by a long shot—but because he'd grown to depend on Bo's closeness at night. He relied on his smiles to brighten his days, his laughter to carry him through the tough times, and his stubborn mothering to keep him going.

Where would he be if Bo left?

"Earth to Adam." Bo waved a hand in Adam's face, his brow popped in question. "You okay, baby?"

To hell with the public. Adam crushed his mouth over Bo's, drinking every ounce of unquestioned courage and strength he offered. Now wasn't the time to worry about Bo leaving. For now, that wasn't a concern. The man he loved might not feel free to love him in return, but he wasn't going anywhere. Of that much, he was sure.

When Adam finally let Bo go, he planted one final kiss on the tip of his nose. "I'm doing great. You ready?"

Bo nodded, reaching out a hand to thread their fingers together. "Lead the way, oh great surprise-bearer."

Adam brought their linked hands to his lips and brushed a kiss over their joined knuckles. Bo had asked for him to plan a night out. Something special to celebrate Lulu passing her first semester of school and Adam making it three-quarters of the way through his training camp. Something he'd promised to let Adam pay for without grumping or groaning.

Which meant Adam had gone all out. He'd gotten them the Presidential Suite at the Bellagio—something Bo had yet to discover, as they hadn't made it to the room—as well as VIP tickets to Cirque du Soleil's O, housed at the Bellagio's main theater. They even had reservations at Michael Mina, also on site. He didn't want to waste a bunch of time walking or cabbing it up and down the Strip. He wanted their night to be special, but he also wanted time to get Bo naked and enjoy all the soft, flat surfaces in their suite.

By the time they'd finished dinner and the show, Adam buzzed with excitement. Thus far, the evening had gone off without a hitch. The dinner had been superb and the show magical. Not the standard result following one of his surprise attempts, but he wasn't about to complain.

As they made their way to the elevator to begin the next leg of their celebration, a couple of tipsy women stumbled into their path. Adam grabbed for Bo to keep him from tripping, but the women crowded their space and forced the two apart.

"Holy friggin' hell, Brittany, I *told you* it was him!" A coppery-haired pixie squealed and clapped her hands together before latching on to Adam's forearm. Her lavender claws dug into his skin. "I am *such* a fan, Mr. Littrell. Like, possibly your biggest. The girls and me? We have tickets to your big fight in a few weeks. We're, like, so friggin' excited to watch you kick that guy's butt."

Adam caught Bo's gaze. He looked dazed but

amused. He tipped his chin in encouragement, and Adam nodded his understanding. The Beast didn't belong outside the ring. If he wanted to interact with his fans, he damn well could. "That's great. I hope it's a good show."

A brunette with long spiral curls bounced in place beside the redhead still clinging to Adam's arm. "We've got one of the two-bedroom suites for the night. It's packed with booze, and Shaina and I *love* to share. Like, everything." The woman, who Adam assumed to be Brittany, waggled her brows. She stroked a knuckle down his bicep. "Why don't you join us? We could have *so much fun.*"

Being nice to a fan was one thing, but tolerating sexual proposals while the man he loved stood only a few feet away was a whole other beast. Rather than slipping into the grumpy asshole he was used to showing the world to get out of their offer, Adam reached around Shaina, grabbed Bo's wrist, and tugged him against his side. "Sorry, ladies, but I'm already taken." With that, he swept a hand behind Bo's back and bent him into an exaggerated kiss.

The two women squealed and giggled. Shaina slapped her palms to her cheeks. "Oh my friggin' hell, that was the most romantic thing I've ever seen."

Brittany sighed and clutched at her friend's arm. "Yeah, if I hadn't already been crushin' on you, it would be over after that. Why are all the good ones gay or taken?"

"Or both, apparently." Shaina grinned.

Adam tucked Bo under his arm and returned the woman's smile. "Why don't you ladies give me your names? If you can make it a bit early, I'll make sure there are some meet-and-greet passes waiting for you after the weigh-in."

It took a few minutes to coordinate, because no one had a pen handy, but Bo finally suggested he put their names in his phone. They took a couple of selfies, and Adam promised to sign something at the weigh-in. Then they were off to find some other poor soul to lure to their hotel room. With any luck, the next one they tried to snare would at the very least be straight, and at the most, not hopelessly in love.

Bo clung to Adam as the elevator carried them to the thirty-third floor of the Spa Tower. "Oh my gosh. Tell me you didn't blow a bunch of money on a superexpensive hotel room." His eyes bugged as the numbers kept climbing. "We aren't going to the penthouse, are we?"

"You didn't think I'd mess around with a cheap room when I had a free pass to do as I pleased without complaint, did you? Come on. You know me better'n that." Adam gave Bo's shoulders a squeeze as the elevator dumped them onto the top floor. The landing that greeted them was contemporary and stylish, yet warm and masculine. Dark wood molding paired with chrome accents and leather in soft cream.

He led Bo down the hall, swiped their room key, and hip bumped the door open. He motioned for Bo to go first and grinned when his gasp strangled into a squeak. "Go on, babe. This is the entryway. There's plenty more where this came from."

"But...." Bo stepped forward, his head swiveling back and forth as he took in the nearly twenty-foot-high walls of water on either side of the foyer. They poured into a small pool separating the foyer from the rest of the suite, crossable only by a walkway suspended above the tranquil basin. "There's a bridge. Adam, there's a *bridge*. Over water. Inside a hotel room. *Our* hotel room."

Chuckling, Adam nudged Bo on. "Go big or go home. You said celebratory. This feels celebratory, doesn't it?"

"Ah, to say the least." Bo swallowed. "I guess it's a good thing we have something pretty big to celebrate, huh?"

Adam let the door close behind them and placed a hand at the small of Bo's back to keep him moving. "I'm so proud of Lulu. I know this has been a rough semester for her. She's still planning on another visit over break, right?"

"Oh, yeah, I mean, yes. It has. And she is. But that's

not what we're *really* celebrating." Bo whistled as he took in the main living area of the suite. "This'll actually work quite nice for the, ah, festivities ahead."

"Oh, I've got quite the *festivities* planned." Adam wrapped his arms around Bo's waist from behind and rested his cheek on the top of his head. "But what are we celebrating if it isn't Lulu's success?"

Bo twisted in Adam's arms until he could snake his own around Adam's middle. "Something I'm guessing you'll be as excited about as I am." He smirked and dug into the back pocket of his jeans, extracting a couple of folded-up pieces of paper. "We got our results."

"Oh fuck." Adam's stomach did a flip. He snatched the papers out of Bo's hand but didn't read them. Instead, he read Bo's face. It provided the answer he'd been hoping for since they'd gone to the clinic together earlier that week. "We're both negative?"

"Yep." Bo flashed an overly toothy grin. "I left the condoms at home and packed the big bottle of lube with all that extra space."

Adam groaned. It wasn't the idea of going bareback for the first time that had his knees going weak, but the fact he'd be inside Bo. *Really* inside him. Skin to skin. They'd be one, if only for that brief period. How could Bo *not* feel his love when they were that close? He might choose to ignore it, but he'd feel it. Deep down, he wouldn't be able to deny it.

And once Bo opened himself to the truth? He'd realize he felt the same way. He had to. They were too perfect together for anything other than forever. Adam just had to sit back and wait. Someday, Bo would be his as much as he was already Bo's.

Chapter Twenty-Two

Everything was perfect. More than perfect, in fact. Adam's surprises always had a way of backfiring a bit, but not tonight. Tonight every piece had fallen right into place.

Even those women—an interruption Bo had dreaded might lead to something negative—added to the flawlessness of the evening. Because, without even meaning to, Adam had spun that encounter into something magical and alleviated Bo's fears with one simple kiss and three little words.

I'm already taken.

After tonight, those words would hold a bit more merit. Six weeks of banging his boss and wanting more— much, *much* more—was six weeks too many. Add the two months prior that he'd spent lusting after him, plus the fact Adam didn't hide his own desires to take their relationship deeper, and it was well past time to make a change.

The problem was, to try for the more they both

wanted meant he'd have to find another job. And considering Bo lived with Adam as a perk of his current position, it also meant finding somewhere else to live.

But Bo didn't care. As long as he could locate a job that paid enough to support himself and Lulu—something he had faith he could manage now he had his GED—he'd do whatever it took to find the freedom to be with Adam.

And what better way to ask a guy to go steady with you than with condom-free sex in a luxurious hotel suite following a fab night on the town?

Bo groaned when Adam's roaming hands slid under his shirt. The sharp contrast of his rough calluses with the soft warmth of his palms and fingertips moving over Bo's back caused goose bumps to prickle his skin. He gripped Adam's shoulders to keep himself upright. "I know there are about a hundred places we could do it in this gi-frickin'-normous place, but I want you in a bed."

"Your wish is my command." Adam's hands disappeared from beneath Bo's shirt, only to reappear a moment later at the back of his thighs. He boosted Bo into his arms so his legs could wrap around that deliciously muscled torso, then swung by the luggage the front desk had delivered and left in the main living space. "Where's that big-ass bottle o' lube?"

Laughing, Bo pointed to the smaller bag. "Front pocket. Didn't want to have to go searching."

Adam planted a loud, smacking kiss on Bo's grinning lips. "You're a god." He kept Bo supported with one arm and hooked his free hand around the handle of the suitcase. "Any preference on beds? I think there are, like, four. Of various sizes."

Bo snorted. "Doesn't matter to me. I just want you spread out and *mine*. All. Mine."

The arm around Bo's lower back tightened. "I'm yours. Always. Any way you want me."

"Then pick a bed and get naked. I need to touch you.

Everywhere."

Adam complied without question. He lugged Bo and the suitcase into the closest bedroom, tossed them both on the bed, and stripped. When Bo rolled off to remove his own clothing, Adam crawled onto the bed in his place and stretched out on his back.

"Put your arms behind your head." Bo wriggled out of his pants and kicked them aside, then tossed his shirt on top. "I don't want you interfering. It's my turn for a little worship session. Well beyond, actually. I don't think I've had you at my mercy for far too many days."

Adam did as Bo requested, reaching back to prop his head on his folded arms. He rolled his hips so every gorgeously carved muscle in his body flexed and moved beneath his skin. "Go 'head, babe. Do your worst."

To avoid any delays when the time came, Bo fished the lube out of the suitcase and tossed it on the bed beside Adam. He edged into the space between Adam's spread legs, running the tips of his fingers featherlight over the tops of Adam's feet all the way to his groin. Adam's breathing increased the farther up Bo's touch crept, and a curse fell from his lips when Bo traced up the underside of his cock.

That big, beautiful cock that would bury deep inside Bo in the very near future with nothing between them but the slick succor of lube.

Bo clenched his jaw. He had to focus. He had to make this special for Adam. Because after, he was going to ask for something that might be hard for Adam to accept. He needed Adam to believe. He needed him to see beyond the obstacles a new job might bring to their relationship. He needed him to accept his need to find a place of his own. To take care of himself and Lulu, and to do so in a way that wouldn't leave them open to disaster if something happened between him and Adam.

He needed Adam to understand that by allowing him the space to step away and find his own footing, he'd only be bringing him closer.

As Bo continued to trail his hands over Adam's body, he reveled in the writhing movement of sinew and muscle that followed in his wake. Adam had been gorgeous from the start, but his added workouts and their increased intensity had done indescribably scrumptious things to his body. Each muscle was cut with precision, standing out in stark relief under the muted bedroom lights. He looked like a sketch from an anatomy textbook. Something an artist dreamt up to represent the ideal of human perfection.

When Bo brushed his thumbs over Adam's nipples, Adam growled and bucked his hips. His eyes flashed with the heat of desire, turning them a dark, stormy gray. "I'm trying really hard to be good here, but I'd like to throw out a little reminder. I haven't come since last night. On a good day, I'd be ready to explode. Then you introduced your little surprise, and...." He groaned. "I'm gonna die. This might be the end for me."

"Oh no you don't. No dying allowed." Bo grinned and gently pinched Adam's nipples between his thumbs and forefingers. As expected—and desired—Adam fired off a round of curses before scooping an arm around Bo's waist and rolling them both so Bo now lay beneath him.

"Tell me to stop and I will." Adam panted against Bo's neck, his voice husky and deep. "But if you don't, I'm gonna make you mine. *Really* mine. All the goddamn way *mine*. No barriers, just us."

Like there was any chance Bo would say anything but, "Yes, please. Do it. *Now*."

Once again, Adam complied without hesitation. He lubed up, gave Bo the minimal amount of prep it had taken Bo *weeks* to convince him was enough, and slipped inside. They both cried out as Adam slid all the way home, pulling Bo into his arms and burying his face in the crook of his neck.

"Jesus Christ." Adam nibbled at Bo's throat. "You

feel like fuckin' heaven. So soft and sweet and *warm*. I'm gonna have to sit here for a minute, 'cause if I move right now? It's over."

"That's okay." Bo hummed in appreciation as Adam kneaded the back of his neck in tandem with the nips, licks, and kisses he rained over his skin. "You can stay like this forever, as far as I'm concerned."

Adam shook his head and rolled his hips in a slow, languorous circle. His cock pressed deeper, and the washboard surface of his abs teased Bo's own dick. The dual zap of pleasure had Bo wilting and tensing all at once. As soon as Adam moved in earnest, it'd be over. Likely for them both.

As if he shared Bo's thoughts, Adam rolled them again so Bo was on top, straddling his hips. Even that minimal movement was enough to leave them both groaning. "I can't be trusted to have control. You've gotta run this show or it'll end way too quick."

Bo clenched his butt and laughed when Adam countered by digging his fingers into Bo's hips and shoving farther inside. He joined their mouths for a delectable kiss, filled with battling tongues and the taste of mutual desire like honeyed wine passing between their lips.

"I… I can't. I need you. I've gotta move." Bo mewled and twisted his hips, driving Adam to respond in kind. They fell into that sweet, cherished rhythm of lovers who knew each other so well, words were no longer needed.

Pressure built at the base of Bo's spine, spreading like molten lava to tighten his muscles and turn his movements desperate and jerky. He grappled at Adam's biceps, finding purchase only at the last second when his orgasm tore through him. He cried out, his back arching as his heart hammered in his ears and his release pooled between them.

Somewhere in the middle of his climactic writhing, Adam joined him. His body tensed, and his cries mingled with Bo's as they shared that ultimate moment of bliss and satiation.

As their breathing slowed and their heart rates evened, Bo lay limp on Adam's chest. His limbs refused to move despite the sticky discomfort driving him to get washcloths for cleanup. Adam's hand moved over his back with slow, comforting strokes that had Bo closing his eyes on a hum.

Now was the time. This was when he needed to tell Adam he wanted more. That he was finally ready to take the next step. That he needed to find another job and leave him so they could truly be together.

But before he could, Lulu's ringtone pierced through the air. Bo froze. She knew what he'd planned for that night. She knew he was going to be with Adam, asking for a commitment, begging for understanding. No way would she call and interrupt unless something was genuinely wrong.

He pushed off Adam's chest, the proof of his release wet and cold on his belly. He pried himself free and snatched his pants off the floor, then dug his phone out of the pocket and slid the answer button to the side before putting the cell to his ear. "Lulu?"

"Ah, hello. Is this Beauregard Wilkins?"

Bo's blood turned to ice, his heart struggling to pump the frozen slush through his veins. "Yes, it is. Who're you? Why are you calling me from my sister's phone?"

Adam appeared at Bo's back. He draped a blanket over his shoulders, then wrapped himself around Bo, holding him close and offering silent comfort and support.

"My name's Mandy. I'm a nurse at Alta Bates's emergency department. Your sister was recently admitted following a motor vehicle accident. Do you live close?"

"Oh God." Bo crumpled under the weight of the woman's words, but he didn't fall. Adam held him up. "I don't, but I can be there in about ten, maybe twelve hours."

Mandy was silent for a moment, then she cleared her throat. "That would be good, Mr. Wilkins. Let the receptionist at the front desk of the emergency room know who you're here to see when you arrive."

"I...." Bo's voice cracked and tears spilled down his cheeks. "I will. Th-thank you."

His fingers went lax and the phone fell to the floor. Adam twisted him in his arms, then pulled him close. He picked up where he'd left off with the gentle caresses over Bo's back. "I'll book us a flight. It'll be faster than driving."

Panic set in, and Bo shook his head. He shoved out of Adam's arms, stumbling over the blanket when it fell from his shoulders. "No. You've got your training camp. You can't miss it."

"Bo." A muscle in Adam's jaw jumped. "I don't give a rat's ass about my training camp. Something's wrong. I'm going with you."

Bo shook his head with more force. "You aren't bailing on your career to chase your personal assistant out to California. I'll be fine."

Adam took a step back, but Bo's focus wasn't on him. He scrambled for his clothes and carried them to the bathroom. All he could think about was renting a car and getting to Lulu. Nothing else mattered.

When he stepped out of the bathroom a few minutes later, Adam had slid on his boxers and held a pad of paper with the hotel's name embossed along the top edge. He handed it to Bo. "That's your flight information. You can print your boarding pass at the airport."

Bo nodded, his eyes roaming the room, looking for what, he had no clue.

"Can I drive you? To the airport?"

"I—" Bo glanced at the words scrawled hastily on the pad. They swam together and scrambled in his brain. He shifted his watery gaze to Adam and crumpled the paper in his fist. "I'd appreciate that."

Chapter Twenty-Three

"What crawled up your ass and died, my man?" Kyle thumped Adam on the back. "Boys are saying you're being more of a shithead than usual. That's saying something, considering you've been slowly turning creampuff on us lately. What spurred the abrupt about-face? Trouble in paradise?"

Adam shot a glare over his shoulder before refocusing his attention on the speed bag. He pounded his fists into the leather and sand with punishing force. "Fuck off."

Kyle chuckled and leaned a hip against the metal frame of the speed bag platform. He watched Adam mistreat the equipment for another couple of minutes before giving his shoulder a shove. "Talk to me, Adam. You're gonna wind up hurting yourself if you don't calm the fuck down and give yourself—and the gear—a break. That poor bag's gonna need restitching when you're done with it."

Grunting, Adam stepped off the platform. Sweat poured down his body, and his muscles—all of them, not just those he'd recently abused at the bag—screamed for reprieve. But he didn't care. What the fuck else was he supposed to do? He couldn't go home. Hell, he couldn't even stop moving. If he did either, Bo haunted his mind.

Adam hadn't heard from him for nearly twenty-four hours after leaving him at the airport. He'd left at least half a dozen frantic messages before Bo had finally called. He'd apologized and said he didn't have a cell phone charger but had borrowed one of the nurse's long enough for a half charge.

Then in a hollow, dead voice, he'd updated Adam on Lulu's situation. She'd been involved in an alcohol-related car accident. Thankfully, she hadn't been the driver, so she faced no legal repercussions, but her injuries were serious. She'd remained intubated in the intensive care unit following a six-hour surgery to address internal bleeding. Another surgery had been planned after she'd further stabilized to repair a fractured femur bone.

That was two days prior. Adam hadn't heard a peep from Bo since. He'd called and left one more message, this time assuring Bo not to worry about finances. He told him to consider himself on indefinite vacation until Lulu was all healed up and promised to send three months' salary in advance to make sure he had funds while he stayed in Cali.

If it were up to him, he'd send Bo every cent in his account and take the next available flight so he could be there to support him in person. But for the time being, all he could do was play by the rules. Bo didn't want that kind of help from him, even if he wanted to give it more than he wanted the air he breathed.

Adam snatched his towel off one of the metal arms on the structure holding the speed bag. He dried his face and the back of his neck before tossing it over his shoulder and rounding to glower at Kyle. "Mind your own business, old man."

Kyle frowned. "I'm sorry, Adam. I feel responsible. I

was the one who pushed Bo on you. Maybe I should've left well enough alone. I just wanted you to be happy."

Sighing, Adam pinched the bridge of his nose. "I was happy. *Am* happy. It'll be okay. Bo's dealing with something right now, and I'm feeling helpless. Once he gets through it, we'll be back to the way we were. I gotta get through this shitty period. Then it'll be good again."

Kyle nodded, but the frown didn't leave his face. He gave Adam's elbow a squeeze. "I give your ass shit, but it's outta love. You know that, right? I'm here if you need me. I can even get mushy if that's where you're at. We can have a few beers and discuss all your fears, maybe even shed a few tears." He beamed. "Check it. I'm a poet and didn't even know it."

"Oh, for fuck's sake." Adam couldn't stop the grin tugging at his lips. "You're a real piece o' work. If I—" He stopped and spun on his heel. Across the room, the cheery boy-band ringtone he'd assigned to Bo blared from his cell. He'd kept his phone on full-blast volume ever since Bo left, something he rarely did. But he wasn't about to miss his call.

Adam bolted through the gym, sidestepping his sparring mate from the day before, who worked on his jujitsu moves with his trainer on a mat between Adam and the lockers. He skidded to a halt in front of the bank of open cubbies most of the guys kept their shit in and grabbed for his bag.

By the time he dug out his phone, the screen flashed a missed call. He cursed and called Bo back, praying to a god he didn't believe in that he'd answer.

"Hey."

Adam swallowed. Bo's voice was so small and distant. He sounded defeated. Broken. Done. "Hey, babe. How're you doing? How's Lulu?"

"She's okay. In a lot of pain, but mostly out of the woods. They're keeping her pretty drugged up."

Bo sniffled, and Adam imagined him huddled into a corner of a cold hospital room, hugging himself. Adam wrapped an arm around his own waist, wishing he could hold Bo. Wishing he could take some of his pain. "Is there anything I can do?"

He almost tacked on a *do you want me to come out there*? but knew better. If Bo wanted him, he'd ask. If not, it would be pressing a subject Bo had already made clear he had no interest in.

"Actually…." Bo sighed. If possible, his voice grew even smaller. "I was calling to see if you'd ship me my things."

Adam sank onto the wooden bench in the locker area. He kept his back to the gym behind him. "Tell me what you need and I'll have it overnighted. I can send you more money too if you need to buy anything while you wait."

A long, painful silence stretched before Bo finally cleared his throat. "I appreciate that. Really, Adam, thank you. But that's not necessary. Pick the cheapest option and I'll pay you back, okay?"

Closing his eyes, Adam nodded even though Bo couldn't see. He wouldn't push him. Not here, not now, not on something they could iron out later. When Lulu was better. When they were back together. "Okay, sure. What do you need? I'll get it out this afternoon."

Again that bone-chilling, agonizing silence ate up the airspace between them. Bo let out a slow, shaky breath. "I need everything. I… I'm quitting. I-I'm not coming back."

"You're not…." Adam's throat closed. He pressed to his feet, his knees wobbly as he stumbled toward the bathrooms. He had to get away. He couldn't break down in public. Especially not to the epic degree he was about to. "You don't have to quit. I told you in my last message, I told you that you could take vacation. For as long as you needed. For as long as it takes to get Lulu better."

"I-I'm sorry, Adam." Bo's words came out broken and strained. "But I have to stay here. I have to focus on Lulu. Not just through her healing, but after too. She's struggling. With life, with school, with everything. She needs me. I… I'm staying here. For good."

Adam rested his forehead on the closed bathroom door. He pressed a hand over the ache in his chest. Tears gathered at the corners of his eyes, but he blinked them back. He couldn't let Bo know how much he hurt. He didn't deserve the guilt that would bring. He was doing the right thing for him and for Lulu, and that's all that mattered. Bo didn't owe Adam anything. He wouldn't let his own pain cause Bo to believe otherwise. He'd be strong for them both. "I understand. If you text me the address, I'll have everything shipped today."

"Okay." Bo's voice was barely a whisper. "Thank you, Adam. I'll send you a check to cover whatever the shipping costs are plus the money you advanced me. I just need a few weeks to find a job. I-if that's okay?"

Clenching his hand into a fist, Adam laid it against the bathroom door where he wished he could punch a goddamn hole through the flimsy particleboard. Instead he schooled his voice to an even keel. "As far as I'm concerned, you're on family medical leave, which is a federally mandated labor law. Take advantage of it for a while, okay? Don't get a job right away. Lulu needs you."

Bo huffed out a breath. "That only applies to businesses with fifty or more employees."

Damn obstinate mule.

A laugh bubbled up Adam's throat and broke on a sob. He tried to play it off with another mirthless chuckle, praying Bo hadn't caught his moment of weakness. "Don't be a pain in my ass, Bo. If nothing else, do it for Lulu. Swallow your stubborn pride and let me help. Just this once. Okay?"

Adam braced himself for another sharp, painful bevy

of words that would break him.

Instead Bo sighed and whispered, "Okay."

It took Kyle about five minutes after Bo hung up to pound down the door. He found Adam on the floor in a puddle of his own sweat and tears. The exact opposite of the beastly image he demanded Adam portray.

Rather than conspire to empty the gym so Adam could sneak out unnoticed or develop some other over-the-top plan to hide Adam's weakness, Kyle crouched on the ground beside him. "I think you've put in a solid day's work. Whataya say we pile into my Jeep and head back to your place? There are some IPAs in your fridge calling our names."

"Might wanna give me a minute." Adam wiped the back of his hand over his cheek. "Can't go out there lookin' like this. The Beast doesn't cry, after all."

Kyle scoffed and slapped a hand over Adam's shoulder. "Fuck 'em. The Beast can do whatever the hell he wants. After beating the record for longest title streak in the history of the UFC, it doesn't matter what you do. Your opponents shit their pants at the thought of climbing into that octagon with you. Whether you show a little human emotion or not, they're still gonna leave brown streaks in their drawers."

Adam snorted and allowed Kyle to pull him to his feet and straight into his arms. He only hesitated a moment before returning the hug and burying his face into the crook of Kyle's neck. Fresh tears threatened, but he bit them back. "Bo's moving to California. He isn't even coming back to get his things. He asked me to ship them to him."

"Oh, Adam." Kyle pressed a strong hand to the back of Adam's head, rubbing the other in a soothing circle over his shoulder blades. "Fuck, I'm so sorry."

Adam shrugged but didn't move from Kyle's comforting, fatherly hold. His dad would never deign to show such physical or emotional support—especially not in public—but Kyle had never shied away from it. He was the father Adam had always wished for. The father his own had never been.

And that's who Bo was to Lulu. Adam couldn't forget that. Maybe he wasn't the father Lulu had always wanted, but he was the only parental figure she had left. He was her rock, her soft place to fall when things got shitty. It made sense for him to be close if she was struggling with life. Adam couldn't fault Bo for the purity of his love for his sister, nor could he even consider asking him to change his mind.

What's done was done. Bo was no longer in his life, and he needed to find a way to accept that. Sooner, rather than later.

Chapter Twenty-Four

"I don't understand why I can't go home with you." Lulu folded her arms and scowled, but the pain behind her grump flashed like angry lightning in her bright blue eyes.

Bo sighed and rubbed at his temple, the sunny yellow of Lulu's rehab room compounding his headache. "There isn't a home to go to right now, Lu. I can't get an apartment until I have a job, and I can't get a job unless I know you're being taken care of. This is a necessary but temporary evil."

"But you *have* a job." Lulu's scowl deepened. She added a pouty lip and huffed out a short, irritated breath. "Adam said you could have family medical leave until I'm healed. Well, guess what, I ain't healed yet."

When Lulu pointed at her casted leg, Bo's stomach flipped. She was far from being healed; that was the truth. Even if he had an apartment, he couldn't take care of her. Not without shelling out big bucks he didn't have for specialized medical and rehab equipment. And the only way he could get those big bucks—or *any* bucks, for that matter—was if he found a job. Which would mean also finding someone to take care of Lulu during the days and evenings, requiring even more money he didn't have.

Adam's offer to keep him on the payroll while Lulu healed was a fortunate one, but it was also inappropriate. He didn't want to take advantage of his good nature. There was no law saying Adam had to keep paying Bo, and by doing so, it forced a connection he would rather see severed. A painful, impossible connection that would lead Adam on if Bo allowed it to continue.

Because no matter how much he wanted things to be different, Lulu's accident had changed everything. She needed him here. After waking up and realizing what had happened, she'd broken down and begged Bo to take her home. She was miserable and confused and didn't want to be out on her own anymore. It was too scary and had led her to make choices she both regretted and feared she'd repeat.

Clearing his throat, Bo shifted his attention back to where it belonged. On his sister, not on the man who refused to leave his head or his heart. Over the past two weeks, despite being hundreds of miles apart and not speaking on the phone once, Bo had failed at his goal of getting over Adam. He'd also made a painful and brutal realization.

He loved Adam. A day late and a couple hundred million dollars short, wasn't he? Even when they'd been together, he hadn't given Adam what he deserved. He'd held back, his focus always on Lulu and never fully on Adam.

Bo placed a gentle hand over Lulu's casted knee. "You not being healed is even more reason a rehabilitation facility is the right place for you right now. I wouldn't be able to take care of you outside of here, especially not if I'm working all hours of the day. They'll be able to do all the things I can't and more."

"Like what? Feed me watered-down Jell-O and get on my last nerve with all their poking and prodding?" She let her head fall to the pillow. Tears swam in her eyes. "I want to go *home*, Bo. Please don't leave me here."

His heart pinched. If it were up to him, he'd never deny Lulu anything. But it wasn't up to him. Not this time. He wasn't equipped to care for her, and at the end of the day, there was no home to bring her back to. The motel he'd used mostly to store his belongings and take an occasional shower over the last few weeks couldn't be mistaken for anything of the sort. And before he could look for a more permanent residence, he needed at least one pay stub to prove he had steady and reliable income.

"I promise I'll start hunting for a job this evening." Bo offered a flat-lipped half smile. "But don't get your hopes up. Cost of living out here is higher than it was back home. Things might be a bit tight for a while, and for now, your school insurance is covering this. We've got to take advantage while we can."

Lulu wiped at her cheeks and sniffled. She kept her gaze locked on the hot pink cast covering her leg from hip to toes. "You can't look for a job tonight."

It would be her first night alone in the rehab facility, but their visiting hours were stricter than the hospital's. He couldn't stay overnight, as he'd been doing there. Still, he could stay as late as they'd allow. "I'll stay here until they kick me out. I promise."

She scrunched her face and peeked a half-squinted eye at Bo. "What about Adam?"

Bo suppressed a sigh. Even in her drugged-up stupor, Lulu had harassed him about calling Adam. She kept insisting he'd want to be with Bo during this "trying time." She also kept reminding him she wasn't stupid. His love for Adam was apparently written all over his face. Long before he'd made the realization for himself, she'd known, and she liked to remind him of that. Endlessly. "What about him?"

"Tonight's his big fight." Lulu raised a brow when Bo winced. "Don't you think you should at least watch? I doubt they've got pay-per-view channels at this fancy place. You should find a bar that's playing it and support him from afar. I'm sure he'd love that. Then report back. Because I'll be dying to find out how hard he creamed his opponent."

He wanted to. He really did. But it was foolish. Not only because he'd left Adam and had no right to continue seeking a connection, but because his fighting terrified Bo. It had been hard enough to see him come home with injuries so frequently. It had been a different matter entirely when Bo had watched him get hurt.

How could he watch an entire fight? Adam was bound to get wounded. In Bo's current high-stress, fragile, and heartbroken state, he'd never survive watching some jerk pound on his boyfriend.

Scratch that. More like *ex*-boyfriend. Or ex... whatever the heck they'd been.

Bo snorted, and Lulu cocked her head in question. What was he supposed to tell her? *Don't mind me, I caught myself referring to my boss as my boyfriend even though I'd never been willing to accept that label despite him begging for that commitment.*

Yeah, no. Not happening. "Adam has plenty of support, Lu. I'm staying here. With you."

She blew out a heavy sigh through her nose and frowned. "Can I get some water?"

Bo leapt to his feet, thankful for a task to distract him. Especially one he could manage. It was hell to feel useless. "Of course. You need or want anything else?"

Lulu shook her head and held out a hand, palm up. "Can I borrow your phone while you're gone? Mine needs a charge, and I want to check my Facebook."

Without thinking, Bo slipped his cell out of his pocket and handed it to her. He scurried from the room, water pitcher in hand, and located the nurses' station. A haggard woman, bent over a stack of papers, pointed him back down the hall he'd come from. The water and ice machine were a few doors down from Lulu's going the opposite direction.

When he got back to his sister's room, she was smirking. He narrowed his eyes and placed the water on the over-bed table. "Why do you look like the rat who got the cheese?"

She shrugged and pressed her lips together, failing at hiding her grin. "I got some fun news. Nothing for you to concern yourself with, big brother."

Rolling his eyes, Bo poured Lulu a glass of water, handed it to her, and flopped into the armchair by her bed. The tiny trip had done jack-nothing to shift Bo's thoughts from Adam. His stomach roiled at the thought of him facing a big fight. Especially alone. Especially when it meant so much and held the power to make or break his career.

If things had been different, Bo would've been there. He would've griped about it and probably lost his lunch—at least twice—out of fear for Adam's well-being, but Adam wouldn't have been alone. He wouldn't be facing such a huge, life-changing moment without someone by his side.

But isn't that how Adam had always approached life? Alone by choice? He had his manager and his coach. They were friends, even if not overly close ones. That's all he'd ever needed, so why did Bo think he'd want anything different now?

Because Adam had done a lot of things with Bo he'd never done before. Things that proved he wanted him for more than the simple ease of having a live-in sex partner with no strings attached. Things that meant something.

Bo groaned and dropped his head into his hands. Why couldn't he stop torturing himself with these thoughts? It didn't matter if Adam cared for him enough to try a real relationship. It didn't even matter if Adam loved him.

With Lulu facing a long and painful recovery, paired with crippling depression and anxiety, Bo's only option was to move to Berkeley. He had to help his baby sister get back on her feet—both literally and figuratively.

Lulu placed one of her small, delicate hands over Bo's. Scabbed-over cuts and bruises marred her skin, as they did nearly everywhere the eye could see. Tears pricked at the back of his eyes when she gave his palm a squeeze.

"Go. You know you want to." She smiled when Bo shifted his gaze to meet hers. "Adam needs you, even if he won't know you're watching. I betcha he'll be hoping you are. This is a big moment for him. Be there, *as a friend*, if nothing else. It's the least you can do for all he's done for us. For giving you the time and money to spend with me in the hospital. For offering to do more if you weren't such a stubborn butt-face and refusing to let him."

Bo pursed his lips, but a chuckle slipped past them anyway. "I'm not the only one who got the old man's obstinate streak."

She flashed a grin and shrugged. "You love me for it. Although yours annoys the crap outta me. *Go*." She waved her hands toward the door. "Don't forget to call and tell me what happened once it's over."

Shaking his head, Bo stood. If the draw of seeing Adam weren't so strong—even a bruised and bleeding Adam who would tear out his heart—Bo would never dream of leaving Lulu. Not on her first night alone in a new and scary place.

But for once, he was going to put himself and his own needs over hers. Not permanently, but for tonight, he'd find a bit of happiness to call his own. And in the morning? He'd find a job. One that paid enough for him to get Lulu and himself a little apartment near campus. And one that, whether his heart wanted him to or not, would allow him to sever ties with Adam. For good.

Chapter Twenty-Five

Adam rolled his neck until it cracked, twice. He glared at Eddie and Kyle, who stood across from him with twin scowls in place. Their irritation was to be expected, but he didn't much care for their two cents. His life choices were his own, whether they agreed with that notion or not. "You two gonna stand there and be grumpy assholes all night?"

Eddie sighed and shot Kyle a side-eye. "What do you expect? Your head isn't in the game. You're gonna get eaten alive out there."

"And if I am? Who fuckin' cares?" Adam pounded a wrapped fist into the palm of his other hand. Maintaining his title was no longer at the top of his priorities list. In fact, ending his career sounded better and better with each passing minute. "I've had a good run. Maybe it's time for someone else to take the title."

"Bull-fuckin'-shit." Kyle strode over to Adam and gave his shoulder a forceful shove. "Since when are you the type to roll over and play dead? You've got a real fuckin' shot at winning tonight if you'd get your head outta your ass."

Adam swung a leg over the bench he'd been straddling and stood, using his height and post-training-camp girth to tower over his manager. "I'm ready to retire, Kyle. You knew it was coming."

"Yeah, when it naturally progressed to that point. Not because you gave up." Eddie folded his arms and leaned against the wall, disappointment written all over his face. "I never thought you'd be one to throw a fight, Littrell."

Adam blew out a breath and shook his head. "I'm not throwing the damn fight."

"You might as well be." Kyle frowned, his own frustration etching lines into his forehead. "Stepping into that octagon without the goal of winning is the same thing."

Kyle wasn't wrong. Adam's drive to win was no longer there. It'd been disappearing for a while now, replaced little by little with the hope for a future with Bo. Watching him walk away hadn't changed the shift in his thought process, especially after the phone call he'd received following weigh-in earlier that day.

The sight of Bo's name flashing across his screen had been enough to turn Adam light-headed and giddy. The last few weeks had been pure torture. A hell unlike any he'd known before. He'd dug into training for the distraction, but his heart hadn't been in it. If either Eddie or Kyle had been paying attention, they would've caught on to his shift in focus long before now.

The caller wound up being Lulu rather than the man he'd hoped for, but the few rushed words she'd spoken brought a grin to his face even now.

According to her, Bo was as miserable as he was and, quite possibly, missed Adam as much. She'd also made it clear she planned to drag her brother's ass back to Vegas. Back to their home and back to *him*.

Her one question, before she'd hissed into the phone that Bo was coming and she had to go, was to ask if Adam would take Bo back if they returned. He hadn't even cared if she meant as his PA or as his lover. He'd said yes, without a doubt.

Which meant, for the first time in two agonizing weeks, he had hope again. Because even if Lulu couldn't convince Bo to move, Adam was going to get his man back. The reason he lived in Las Vegas in the first place was his UFC career. If that was over, he'd be free to live anywhere. And if Bo would have him, he wanted that anywhere to be wherever Bo called home, be it Berkeley, Las Vegas, or parts yet unknown.

If he could get Bo back in his life—for good—Adam would move to the North fuckin' Pole, for all he cared. The location didn't matter, only the company.

"I'm not gonna actively try to lose, but I'm not gonna kill myself either. I'll give a solid effort, but if Zaragoza brings the passion I've seen in our training videos, the belt belongs to him." Adam adjusted the groin protector beneath his fight briefs. Errant images of Bo in the throes of his own passion had it fitting a bit tight. "If he wants it more than I do, he deserves it."

Eddie huffed out a mirthless laugh. "The better fighter is who deserves it, Littrell, and you're a better fucking fighter."

Outside the locker room, Adam's arrival was announced. The familiar echo of the exaggerated voice boomed and bounced through his head for what he hoped would be the last time. A moment later, his entrance song blared into the packed MGM Grand Garden Arena.

He took a step forward and clapped his manager and coach on the shoulders, giving them both a conciliatory squeeze. "It's been an adventure, boys, but I think it's high time we lay the Beast to rest."

Adam groaned when the peal of his doorbell reverberated through his pounding head. He didn't budge off the couch, where he'd taken to sleeping after Bo left. Instead he willed the unwelcome visitor away and cursed them with every foul word his aching brain could generate when the bell rang a second time.

Pushing to his feet, Adam swayed and grabbed for the arm of the couch. He pressed a gentle hand to the side of his head, where Zaragoza had damn near knocked the thing off his shoulders, and suppressed a wave of nausea by puffing out his cheeks and holding his breath.

Going to the hospital for a scan like his coach—now *ex*-coach—had suggested might've been a good idea. It wasn't like Adam had never had a concussion before, but he was getting on in age, and the more of the damn things he suffered, the riskier they were. And there was no doubt he'd been concussed. Even if Adam had set out to win, it was unlikely he would've succeeded. Zaragoza—fifteen years Adam's junior and built to the top of the weight class—had entered the fight guns blazing.

The fuckin' chime clanged through his brain a third time. Adam glowered at the door. It was only a few yards away, but in his present state, it might as well be hundreds of miles. He shuffled to the foyer and gave the door a yank, fully prepared to bitch out whoever stood on his porch.

Until he saw who it was.

"Holy crap." Bo's eyes bugged behind his glasses. He stepped forward, and before Adam had a chance to prepare himself, those soft, familiar hands cupped his jaw. "Why didn't anyone dress this? Have you at least been using ice?"

"Ah, no." Adam rolled his lips in to hide a smile when Bo's brows pinched at his response. Some things never changed. Bo was built to fret and mother.

Bo ran a gentle thumb over Adam's cheekbone. His

left eye was damn near swollen shut, and if the blood crusted over his face the last time he'd looked in the bathroom mirror meant anything, he had at least a few open wounds. Eddie had come after him with the first aid kit following the fight, but Adam had refused his care. He'd wanted to go home. Prepared to retire or not, the severe beating he'd taken had dealt more than physical damage. His ego had been smarting, as well.

"And why not?" Bo tutted and lowered his hands. He grabbed one of Adam's wrists, tugging him toward the kitchen. "Hasn't anyone been looking after you since I left?"

Adam obeyed when Bo pointed to a chair and ordered him to sit. He bit his split and swollen bottom lip to stop the ridiculous grin threatening to pull at the corners of his mouth. "Eddie tried. I wouldn't let him."

"Of course you wouldn't," Bo grumbled as he dug through the cupboard he'd cleared and stocked with a myriad of first aid supplies all those months ago. "And you call me stubborn."

A chuckle slipped free before Adam could stop it. "You are stubborn."

Bo rolled his eyes as he approached Adam with a fistful of bandages and tubes of antibiotic and pain-relieving creams. He placed his booty on the table beside Adam before retrieving one of the premade ice packs he kept stocked in the freezer. He offered it to Adam, one brow raised. "Hold this wherever it hurts."

"We're gonna need a lot more ice if that's the only specification." The grin he'd tried to hold back stretched his lips into a smirk when Bo's brow crept farther up his forehead. He accepted the ice and pressed it to his temple like a good boy.

Seemingly satisfied with Adam's cooperation, Bo shifted his attention to the items on the table. He opened bandages and uncapped the various liniments before tugging over a chair so he could sit facing Adam. He frowned.

"Cheese and rice, Adam. You look like crap."

"I never claimed to be pretty." Adam chuckled, dropping his ice pack at Bo's silent behest so he could tend the cut over his eye.

When Bo signaled him to return the ice to his swollen face a few minutes later, Adam obliged. "Can I ask what you're doing here? Not that I'm complaining, but...." He shrugged. How did he tell the man he loved he hadn't been sure he'd ever see him again? Least of all back in his kitchen. In Vegas. Without his sister. "Wait, where's Lulu?"

Had she succeeded in talking her brother into moving already? No, that wasn't possible. For as damaged as she'd sounded, the move would be a difficult one. Not something Bo could make happen overnight.

Which meant what? Why was Bo here?

Adam shifted in his seat, his stomach dropping when Bo averted his gaze and busied himself with cleaning up bandage wrappers rather than answering Adam's questions. "Bo?"

Bo sighed, darting his eyes to meet Adam's. He swallowed and offered a weak smile. "Lulu's in rehab, and I...." He mirrored Adam's own helpless shrug. "I saw your fight last night. I-I was worried about you. I know how much it meant to you to keep your title, and I... I didn't want you to be alone."

Adam's heart slammed to warp speed beneath his ribs, and his stomach did a delighted flip back to rights. He glanced at the digital clock on the microwave, noting the hour for the first time. It was only a little after nine o'clock. Considering the main card event—his and Zaragoza's title brawl—hadn't started until 10:00 p.m., Bo had either hopped an early flight—which was unlikely, considering his penny-pinching ways—or driven all night long. And he'd done so because he cared about Adam enough not to want him to face the loss of his title alone.

Before Adam could formulate a proper response that

didn't entail the profession of his undying love and a lot of teary-eyed begging for Bo to take him back, Bo bounced to his feet like a loaded spring. "Coffee. You need coffee. Why isn't your coffee pot programmed to make it automatically anymore? You can't function without it."

Adam huffed out a laugh. "It kept brewing sludge rather than anything resembling coffee, because I can never remember to add water or replace the filter and grounds. So I turned the damn thing off."

Bo readied the machine and turned it on before easing back to his seat. He fiddled with one of the ointment tubes and cast his eyes to the floor. "If you'd rather I leave—"

"Fuck no." Adam dropped the ice pack to the table with a dull thud. He leaned forward and took Bo's warm hands in his nearly frozen grip. "I was just wondering. I hadn't anticipated finding you on my porch this morning. It's a welcome surprise, but an unexpected one. That's all."

Bo gave Adam's hands a squeeze and scooted forward on his chair. His brilliant green eyes locked on to Adam's. "I've missed you. So frickin' much."

That was all Adam needed to hear. "Me too, babe. Me fuckin' too." He pulled Bo into his lap and buried his battered face in the soothing familiarity of Bo's neck. Bo snaked his arms around Adam's ribs and blew out a gentle sigh.

Everything was perfect. Adam's injuries disappeared, as did the distance and time that had separated them. His only care in the world was the comfort of Bo's slender warmth and the steady rise and fall of his chest, serving as proof Bo was alive. He was real.

In that moment, nothing else mattered, and anything that did could bloody well fuckin' wait.

Chapter Twenty-Six

Bo soaked up Adam's strength and warmth for as long as he could before pulling away to lock his gaze on those beautiful gray irises. He brushed a knuckle beneath the bandage he'd placed over the worst of Adam's injuries and frowned. He'd been right when he'd assumed watching Adam get beat on would break him. Despite being at a public bar, surrounded by people, tears had flooded his cheeks.

And that was before the final round, when the referee had ended the fight by announcing Adam's loss. Standing there, bloodied and bruised, Adam had accepted defeat like the champ he truly was. But under his stoic exterior, through the eyes of a lover who knew him well, the heartache was clear.

Bo hadn't thought twice. He'd sent Lulu a text to tell her Adam lost, and before he could send another to let her know he'd be leaving for a few days, she'd responded with, *Drive careful and pull over if you get tired. Let me know when you get to Vegas safe and sound. Oh, and give Adam a hug for me.*

How could he leave Adam here to face that pain on his own? Just because they'd been forced apart by things outside their control didn't mean Bo loved him any less. He hadn't even realized how deeply he cared for Adam until their separation forced him to step back. When he looked at everything he'd taken for granted during their time together—everything Adam had tried to offer but he'd refused—driving to Vegas had been the only logical response. Leaving Adam to suffer alone was out of the question.

"I'm so sorry, Adam." Bo clenched his jaw as shame turned his stomach sour. "About everything. About leaving the way I did and about not coming back to get my stuff myself. Calling you like that and making you do it when I hadn't spoken to you in days was…. I've been a jerk and a—"

Adam placed a finger over Bo's lips. "It's okay. You did what you had to do to take care of yourself and your sister. There's nothing wrong with that. Your priorities were in the right place."

Maybe they were, but that didn't mean Bo had handled things well. He'd fled right on the brink of securing a commitment he knew Adam wanted as much as he did. Rather than letting him help, Bo had pushed him away. He'd been a selfish coward. Too focused on his own issues to realize what his actions might've done to Adam.

"Part of that hug was from Lulu, by the way." Bo wriggled in Adam's hold when Adam cocked a brow and bumped his hips to highlight their mutual hard-ons. "I mean, the G-rated upper-body portion. Everything down south was *all* me."

Adam laughed. The deep, familiar tenor washed over Bo in a comforting wave. The loneliness and misery of the past few weeks disappeared, replaced by that special brand of security, solace, and cozy contentment he only felt in Adam's presence.

"How is the little monster? She sounded well enough when we spoke yesterday, but—"

"Wait, you two talked yesterday? When? How? She doesn't even have your.... Oh." Bo's shoulders sagged, and he shook his head. A smile crept up his lips. "That little pain in my butt. She borrowed my phone to check her Facebook because hers was dead, then sent me to get her ice water. I never thought she'd use it for anything other than the stated purpose or I wouldn't've given it to her."

Chuckling, Adam ran his callused hands up and down Bo's arms. "She seemed a bit rushed. That's probably why, eh?" He grinned. "So that means you don't know why she called, do you?"

"No, but I can guess." Bo sighed and climbed off Adam's lap. The coffee was done, so he poured them both a steaming mugful and joined Adam back at the table. On his own chair this time. "She's antsy to get out of the sterile hospital environment and back home. Unfortunately I've been living out of a motel, so there really isn't a 'home' to go back to yet. I told her I'd need to find a job before getting an apartment, and she of course argued I already had one."

Bo glanced at Adam and cringed at the smirk on his face. Just as he suspected. The little brat had circumvented him and called Adam to plead for an extension to his kindness. Something Bo did *not* want. He had a GED and a solid work history. He could and *would* find a job that, even with California's high cost of living, could support them. It wasn't Adam's responsibility to keep throwing money their way. "I'm sorry. Lulu's never been great at discerning boundaries or recognizing when they shouldn't be crossed."

Adam threaded his fingers with Bo's, drawing their joined hands to his lips for a kiss. "Have you talked to Lulu about what she wants? Aside from getting out of the hospital environment, that is."

Electricity fired under Bo's skin at the feel of Adam's

lips. He struggled to get his mind out of the king-sized bed upstairs and back to the topic at hand. Clearing his throat, he slid his gaze to meet Adam's and focused on the soft warmth of his stare. "She's having trouble at school. The excessive alcohol intake was more a symptom of that than anything else. I think she needs a stable environment right now. She wasn't quite ready to be out on her own, especially so far from home and... well, me. We've relied on each other nearly our whole lives, you know?"

Adam ran his thumb over their linked knuckles in gentle circles. He tipped his head to the side. "Does she want to stay in Berkeley?"

"What, you mean stay in school?" Bo scrunched his brow. "Of course she does. She was so excited about getting into UC Berkeley. It was her dream for most of high school."

"Was? Or is?" Adam offered a soft smile. "I kinda got the impression she wanted to come back to Vegas. Has she said anything to you?"

Lulu told Adam she wanted to move back to Las Vegas?

Bo rubbed at the back of his neck with his free hand, his stomach doing a delighted flip when Adam offered one of his most adorable lopsided grins. How had he endured the past two weeks without the man who could right all his wrongs with a single smile? Even more pressing of a question, how could he survive the rest of his life without him?

"Lulu said that? That she wants to move back?"

Adam shrugged. "Not in so many words, but she did say she planned to drag you back here. To Vegas... and to me." He cleared his throat, and a slight tinge of pink colored his cheeks. "She wanted to know if I'd take you back. I didn't bother to ask what capacity she referred to because the answer would be the same either way."

Bo swallowed, his heart thrumming to life in an erratic rhythm. His pulse jumped at his throat. What was Lulu's game? She couldn't be trying to get rid of him. If nothing else, she'd made it clear she wanted to be with Bo and she wanted to go home. "Oh. Crap."

Lulu hadn't wanted Bo to mooch off Adam. Her goal hadn't been for him to soak up a salary while living hundreds of miles away doing nothing to earn it. She'd wanted him to keep his job in Vegas because she wanted to go *home*. Not to an apartment in Berkeley where she'd spiraled into depression, but to the place she'd lived happily all her life. To the place she and Bo belonged.

Giving Adam's hand a squeeze, Bo slipped his fingers free. He dug his cell out of his pocket and shot Lulu a text. He waited, on the edge of his chair, until she replied. Barely twenty seconds later. He could almost hear the eye roll in her words when he read, *Took you long enough, genius. Yes, I want to move home. TO VEGAS.*

"Everything okay?"

The note of concern in Adam's voice brought a grin to Bo's lips. He tossed his phone on the table and crawled back into Adam's lap, thrilled when Adam's mouth stretched to match his own goofy smile.

"Sounds like I'm moving home." Bo laughed when Adam's beaming face cracked even further, his gray eyes sparkling with delight. "Mind telling me what your answer was? It's imperative I know now."

Adam cocked an inquisitive brow. "My answer?"

"To Lulu's question. The one you didn't deign to get the specifics on because the answer would be the same either way."

"Oh, *that* answer." Adam smirked and gave Bo's backside a squeeze, tugging him closer. "It was a resounding yes."

Bo rolled his hips so their cocks grazed. They both moaned and the hold Adam had on his butt strengthened, his eyes turning smoky with desire.

He hadn't thought he'd have another opportunity to

broach the subject he'd meant to discuss in the hotel all those weeks before, but presented with a second chance, Bo found himself wavering.

He didn't want to remain Adam's PA. Of that much, he was sure. He needed to find employment elsewhere. Something outside their relationship that could support him and Lulu while allowing him and Adam to date. Unhindered. Without any undue risk to his financial stability or any unnecessary guilt for Adam.

If their relationship didn't work, they both needed the freedom to step away without any negative consequences. Otherwise, how could they trust the other wasn't sticking around to avoid hardship or discomfort?

But it wasn't his employment status that had Bo pausing. Adam would agree to those terms easily enough. It was the thought of moving back to Vegas and living apart from Adam. The very idea made his skin crawl. After living together for so many months, this house felt like home to him. Especially when he got to sink into bed with the man he loved every night.

But could Lulu find herself a home here?

More importantly, would Adam want her to?

"Babe?" Adam knuckled under Bo's chin, forcing their gazes to meet. "Talk to me. I can see your gears turning. Don't shut me out. Let me help. What's got you worried?"

Bo licked his lips, taking a moment to relish the flash of longing that darkened Adam's eyes as a result. He laced his fingers behind Adam's neck and rubbed his thumbs into his hairline. When Adam closed his eyes and purred, the knot of nerves in Bo's belly loosened. "What if I told you I don't want to come back as your PA?"

Adam squinted one eye open, cringed, then opened them both. "I'd say I'm not surprised. I'd also fully support any decision you feel is right for you, but I'd ask you to consider allowing me to keep you and Lulu comfortable until she's better. Now isn't the time to be starting a new gig. Lulu needs you here, at home, helping her heal. We can get some home health nurses to come during the day, but she needs her brother too. Her healing isn't going to be purely physical, after all. She's been through a lot."

Bo's pulse quickened. He tightened his hold on the back of Adam's neck. "And by 'home,' you mean—"

"Here." Adam's faced hardened. "I mean here. In our home. Just because you went to Berkeley to take care of Lulu for a few weeks doesn't mean this isn't still your home. I want you and Lulu to move in with me for good. I love you, and for some insane reason, that darling little monster has grown on me too. But don't tell her that. I enjoy our sparring."

"Yeah, when you aren't breaking my eardrums with your painful attempts at harmonization." Bo chuckled, the sound choking at the back of his throat when realization dawned on him like a brick falling square on his head. He let his hands fall from Adam's neck to rest on his shoulders, then squared his own. "Cheese and rice, Adam, you can't drop a nuclear bomb and act like the world didn't tilt on its frickin' axis as a result."

Adam drew back his chin and inclined his head to the side. "Asking you to move back in is a nuclear bomb?"

Bo snorted. "No, but saying 'I love you' sure is."

When Adam turned ashen, his eyes popping and jaw dropping comically wide, Bo grinned. So it hadn't been a purposeful admission. Who cares? It needed to be said. Bo had hoped he felt the same—had all but convinced himself he did—but hearing the words spoken aloud did strange and wonderful things to his insides. He gave Adam's shoulder a gentle shove, careful not to put any real pressure in case there were hidden bruises. Which there undoubtedly were. "Don't worry, I love you too, you big squishy-hearted oaf."

Adam growled and thrust to his feet. Bo squealed,

latching on with all four limbs at the sudden shift in his equilibrium. Not that Adam would ever let him fall. Not that Bo could ever think he would.

"Can I take you to bed?" Adam's voice was gruff, husky with desire. "I think it's time we made love. Proper like."

Bo rocked his hips and groaned. "I thought you'd never ask."

Chapter Twenty-Seven

Adam slid into bed with Bo still clutching on to him like a monkey. A ridiculously sexy, far-too-clothed monkey. A few of his bruises twinged at the disservice, but he ignored them. The only thing he cared about at that moment was getting Bo undressed. He needed to touch him and feel the warmth of his skin against his own.

Bo clawed at Adam's T-shirt, panting, writhing, and whimpering. "Naked. Now."

"As you command, my love." Adam winked and extracted himself from Bo's needy grip. He yanked off his T-shirt and reached for Bo's, giving it a tug before realizing the other man had gone still beneath him. "Bo?"

"Oh, baby." Bo's face pinched, and he touched a tentative fingertip to a purple welt on Adam's ribs. Only one of many. Nothing he wasn't used to following a full-out fight, but Bo had never seen him this banged up. They wore more protective gear and tended to cut each other a little slack in the practice ring, but it was a brawl to the death in the octagon. Under all those stage lights, surrounded by the roar of a crowd who hungered for blood and pain, no one held back.

Not even a smart-mouthed old fuck who claimed he didn't want to win. Especially in the face of an angry, ferocious opponent out to hand his balls to the highest bidder. Adam's natural defenses had kicked in almost immediately, which meant he'd given it his all. Zaragoza's win had been hard-fought and well-earned.

"I'm fine, babe." Adam gave Bo's shirt another tug. "I haven't had my hands on you in weeks. What I need right now is you. *All* of you. Don't you dare hold back or go easy on me."

Bo laughed when Adam pulled at his shirt yet again. He raised his arms and allowed the piece of clothing to be removed before laying a sober gaze on Adam. "I won't hurt you."

Rolling his eyes, Adam hopped from the bed and dropped his drawers. "You aren't gonna hurt me. I'm the Beast. The Beast eats pain for breakfast." That, and Adam was used to going about his daily life pretending to be fine, even after a brutal fight. He was used to pushing through the pain.

To rest on your laurels is to admit defeat. It was a phrase his father uttered frequently, and one that had stayed with him all these years. He'd never let Adam rest, no matter the circumstance.

Pleasing his old man, while a ridiculous goal, had always been something Adam strived for. Giving up that stress to be perfect, to perform to his father's exact specifications, would be one of many benefits to his retirement. The best of which lay sprawled on the bed before him, still unacceptably half-clothed.

"Help a brother out, would you?" Adam gave Bo's jeans a yank. "Undo the fly. These puppies have gotta go."

Bo complied, a small smile curving his lips. When he was finally naked, he stretched out his arms and Adam slipped into them. Their bodies molded together like two parts of the same puzzle, cut into jagged, messy pieces made to fit one within the other.

Despite the incessant urges driving him to grind his long-deprived cock against the supple warmth of Bo's welcoming body, Adam lay still. As did Bo. An unspoken swell of emotion passed between them, and their grips tightened.

"I love you, baby." The words came out muffled, as Bo's face was buried in Adam's neck, but they were clear enough to send a zing of unfettered joy straight into Adam's heart.

He pulled away enough to give Bo space to tip his head at Adam's urging. When their eyes met, Adam's heart swelled even further. Bo blinked at him with tears glistening on his lashes, his glasses smudged and askew. Adam removed the frames, setting them aside before stroking his thumb over Bo's cheek to collect a single escaped tear. "I love you too, Beauregard Wilkins."

Bo sighed, smiling drunkenly. "That sounds mighty nice."

"Mmm." Adam hummed his agreement, finally rocking his hips to assuage the rampant hunger aching through his groin and belly. "Make love to me. I want our first time, like this, to be special. I want to feel you inside me."

Bo froze, his eyes widening. "I've never… I mean, *you've* never either, right?"

Chuckling, Adam rolled them so he was flat on his back and Bo straddled his hips. "No, I've never been the receiver. I've never wanted that before, but I've dreamed of doing it with you. I want us to be equals—in all things—and that starts here. In bed." He ran both hands up Bo's thighs, enjoying the strained whimper that followed. "I want you to claim me, as I did with you in that hotel. Skin to skin, heart to heart. I want to be yours."

"I won't last two pumps at this rate." Bo panted out the words, resting his weight on shaky arms, his palms seated over Adam's pecs. "Maybe we should wait until—"

"No way." Adam took Bo's leaking dick in hand, giving it a few gentle tugs that sent Bo's back arching and a slew of incoherent mumbles tumbling from his lips. "Unless you're opposed to the idea—which is 100 percent okay, you can *always* say no—then I want you buried inside me when you come. I don't care if it's three seconds, three minutes, or three hours."

He meant every word. He'd dreamt of finding that unique connection with Bo since far too early in their relationship. The desire to be filled by another man had never been one to pique his interest, nor had it ever been anything requested of him. Quite the opposite. The Beast was always expected to be dominant and in control.

But with Bo? Adam wanted to give as much as he received. He wanted their love to find equal footing, not follow stereotypes and demands only fit for the outside world. In their little bubble, they could be and do whatever they wanted. And Adam wanted to give Bo the gift of vulnerability. Both his own and Adam's.

Bo placed a gentle hand around Adam's wrist and pulled, a delightful little groan toppling from his lips when Adam released his cock following the silent demand. With trembling guidance, he moved Adam's hand to his own dick, wrapping their joined hands around it and returning the sweet, tormenting favor with a few pointed strokes. When he used his other hand to cup and knead Adam's balls, Adam clenched his jaw and garbled out a moan.

Smirking, Bo kept up the actions, rocking his hips in time with the movement of their linked hands. "Can you reach the lube?"

Chest heaving as he struggled to catch his breath, Adam nodded. He reached blindly for the nightstand, knocking several items to the floor with a loud crash before finding the handle to the top drawer and giving it a forceful jerk. Thankfully, the lube was on top. He snatched it free and tossed it on the bed by Bo's knee.

Bo unthreaded their fingers and raised a brow when Adam let his hand fall to his side. "This is gonna be quick, baby. I need you as close to that edge as possible so I stand some semblance of a chance at making you feel good. You keep working toward that goal while I get us prepped."

Laughter—strained, horny, ridiculous laughter—bubbled up Adam's throat. If Bo had any idea how much effort he'd put into *not* coming over the past few minutes, he'd be making much quicker work of that lube job. "Babe, I'm thirty-eight. Not outta my prime yet, but no spring chicken either. Trust me, if you think *you've* got it bad, that's nothing compared to where I'm at. If I hadn't been running multiplication tables at the back of my mind for the past ten minutes, that request would be pointless. Trust me, I'm on edge. I'm very, very on edge."

Bo cracked a grin, his flushed face lighting up like it was Christmas fuckin' morning. "Well, thank goodness for all the GED prep. I told you memorizing those multiplication tables would be beneficial eventually."

"Yeah, it's gone a long way toward increasing the value of my sex life, if nothing else. It'd be a shame if I blew my load before the man I loved got his beautiful dick inside me, now wouldn't it?" Adam smirked, obliging Bo's silent request to bend his knees. When that first press of lube-slickened fingers met his ass, rubbing in small, gentle circles, he closed his eyes and hummed with pleasure. "Go 'head. I'm ready."

There was a low grunt, followed by an increase in pressure as Bo's fingers slid inside. He worked them slowly in and out while Adam focused on breathing. It wasn't a sensation he was used to, but it wasn't an unpleasant one. Especially not when Bo twisted his hand, crooked his fingers, and stroked. A jolt of molten pleasure radiated from somewhere deep within Adam's groin. "Holy fuckin' shit."

Bo chuckled. "Now you see why I have absolutely zero issues with being a bottom. Just wait. It gets better—at least for me—when you're filled to the brim and getting stimulated from every possible angle. Including these delicious abs grating against my dick."

When Bo's fingers trailed over Adam's stomach, he blew out a breath and gripped his wrist. A hint of desperation he didn't even try to hide laced his words when he spoke. "Please. Take me. Give me that. Give me *everything*."

It was selfish of him to demand such things. To ask Bo to give so much when he had every intention of simply lying there and taking it. But that's how it worked. The give and take weren't always equal at first, but they always were by the end.

Bo pulled his fingers free, the empty sensation that followed a strange and needy one. Adam shifted his hips, fisting his hands into the comforter beneath him to stop himself from flipping Bo over and taking what his body so desperately wanted. Because it wasn't about gaining release wherever his ravenous, rutting cock could find it. It was about the very basics of love, of sharing mutual pleasure, and of cherishing the man who owned his heart.

With shaky, uncertain movements, Bo lined himself up at Adam's entrance, raised a questioning brow to be sure Adam was ready—which he so fucking was—and pressed home.

Adam released his death grip on the comforter and instead wrapped his arms around Bo, pulling their bodies flush. His bottom lip was split, swollen, and tender—the only reason he hadn't stolen a kiss and likely why Bo hadn't tried, either—but when his heart filled near to bursting at their connection, he couldn't give two shits about a little pain. He slid a palm behind Bo's neck and brought their mouths together, groaning when Bo opened for him without question.

Then he moved. Sweet, delicious little hip rolls that sent a shock of decadent desire through every nerve ending in Adam's body. Bo was right. There was nothing quite like the feeling of being filled by the man you love, with every possible pleasure point stimulated in unexpected and delightful ways.

Bo tore his lips from Adam's. He scrunched his face into a determined scowl. "Crap. I told you I wouldn't last...."

"Go ahead, babe. Come for me." Adam's voice was husky, a testament to his own strained attempt at control. If Bo let go, so could he.

Nodding, his breath coming in ever-shortening gasps, Bo arched his back, dug his nails into Adam's chest, and cried out as his release shuddered through his body. Adam clung to the edge a moment longer, only enough to revel in the beauty of Bo's surrender, then fell right along with him.

Bo was the first to move. He peppered kisses over every inch of Adam's exposed flesh he could reach, then shoved to his hands. He grinned, mirth sparkling in the emerald gems of his eyes. "I'll make you a deal."

"Okay." Adam drew out the word, a smile of his own pulling at his swollen lip. "Shoot."

"I'll move my bratty, pain-in-the butt sister into your—no, sorry, *our*—home. I'll even let you shell out money to keep me here with her until she's well enough that I can get another job, but only on one condition."

Adam's heart, still struggling to settle to its normal speed, thumped with renewed vigor. "Name it and it's yours. Anything. *Every*thing."

Bo's grin turned wicked. He thrust his hips where their bodies still connected, sending a zing up Adam's spine. "You've gotta let me do that again. Maybe more than once."

"Oh, babe." Adam guffawed, drawing Bo back into his arms. "We can do that every time if you want. Anytime you want."

Bo snorted. "No way. I'm not giving up the pleasures of being a bottom. How about we take turns?"

"Fair enough, but there is one area of concern I'd like to address." Adam brushed a kiss over the crown of Bo's head when he simply hummed in question. "While Lulu's living here, can we relax the rules? At least a little?"

"The rules?" Bo lifted his head and pinched his brow. "What rules?"

Laughing, Adam pressed a thumb over the crinkled V on Bo's forehead and rubbed it smooth. "The sleeping fully clothed and no sex rules."

"Oh, screw that." Bo let his head drop and nuzzled into Adam's neck. "Like you said, Lulu's a big girl. She knows what happens between two people who love each other. We can buy her earplugs or a really loud speaker system."

Adam gave the comforter a tug, pulling the free end over Bo's back so they were nestled under its warmth. They were sticky and needed to clean up, but that could wait. For now, he was going to enjoy holding Bo close and relish the wide-open brightness of their future. Because together, no matter what life might throw their way, Beauregard and the Beast had already found their happily ever after.

Epilogue

Four and a Half Years Later

"I can't believe my baby sister is graduating college."
Bo sniffled, swiping at the steady stream of happy tears
spilling down his cheeks. He settled into Adam's warm
embrace, resting his head on Adam's shoulder as the endless
mass of graduation-gown-clad students shuffled into position on the University of Nevada football field.

"That'll be you soon, babe." Adam gave Bo's arm a
squeeze. "One more year."

It still sent tingles racing up Bo's spine to think he'd
have a college degree someday. A dual bachelor's in history and English, no less. Considering he'd made it to twenty-five without getting his GED, the dream of college had
always been that. A dream.

A dream Adam had helped turn into reality. Not
only by teaming up to get their GEDs, but also by standing
by his side and supporting him through everything since.

The trials and tribulations associated with Lulu's long, agonizing recovery. The battles they'd waged to get her back into school and then eventually back out on her own. The tears and guilt Bo faced after both.

But it hadn't all been bad. Anything but, in fact. The nearly five years since Adam Littrell had entered Bo's life were by far the best he'd ever had. Adam understood him. He didn't fight Bo's needs or wants, even when they were ridiculous. He supported him unconditionally and had from the start. It had just taken Bo a little longer than Adam to realize what they had.

Once he did? There was no looking back. Their love grew stronger every day, held up by their shared experiences, both the triumphs and the failures.

It had been Adam's suggestion that Bo go to college. After he'd settled into a gig at a local bookstore, one that eventually turned into a managerial position he still held and cherished to this day, Adam had nudged him into applying. He'd known Bo had always wanted to but was observant enough to realize he'd never consider it on his own. It was something he'd viewed as a selfish extravagance.

But that's where Adam swooped in to save the day, yet again. As a gift to Bo, and to Lulu of course, Adam had set up a trust in her name. It covered not only her schooling, but also "incidentals" like rent, food, and books.

It'd been difficult for Bo to accept at first. It felt like charity, and he feared it would build animosity between them and put what they had at risk. But that was early in their relationship, before he accepted how pure of heart Adam truly was. He'd done it because he wanted to and because he *could*, but also because he knew Bo would always worry about Lulu. By setting up that trust, he'd essentially taken that financial burden off Bo's back and given him the freedom to make decisions for himself, rather than fretting how they'd affect her.

Which meant he'd latched on to the idea of going

back to school and run with it. He'd even accepted yet another generous gift from Adam—a trust in his own name to cover the costs of his degree. It'd been another hard sell, but Adam could be surprisingly persuasive. And insanely patient.

Two skills that went a long way toward building his own fledgling career. After retirement, Adam had floundered for a while. He'd focused on Bo and Lulu, but it was clear he was adrift without the structure of his daily workouts and training schedules. It wasn't like he quit exercising, but there was no endgame in sight. That part of him that had spent every day since he was a young teen building toward the next fight, the next win had been left gutted and empty.

Bo had understood that sentiment far too well. After spending years as an uneducated grunt worker, with no purpose to his profession but putting food on the table, he'd thrived at the bookstore. It was his calling. Something he loved and that added to his happiness. He knew where Adam's head was because that's where he'd parked his brain for the first half of his twenties.

It was quite by chance Adam stumbled into his current gig. About three months after Lulu's accident, he'd taken over her home-based rehab. He went with her to all her appointments while Bo was at work and helped her do the exercises safely and effectively at home. It was Lulu who'd suggested Adam put his training skills and endless patience to good use.

A few months later, Adam had opened his own gym. It focused on the youth population rather than adults, and he'd even started a program for underprivileged kids and teens so they could join the gym without a financial strain on their families. It provided them a safe place to go after school and included all the necessary equipment, clothing, and a healthy snack every day to get them through until dinner.

Four years later, Adam's gym had grown so successful, and his after-school program so beneficial to the community, he'd opened two other locations and garnered unsolicited grant money to beef up the charitable side.

"There she goes, babe." Adam hugged Bo's shoulders. "Our little monster, all grown up and a big-time college grad."

Bo beamed as the speakers boomed, "Tallulah Wilkins, bachelor of arts in computer science." It was a stretch from her original goal of mechanical engineering, but Lulu had fallen in love with the technical side of her degree. So much so that she already had a job lined up with the company she'd interned for as a computer programmer helping to develop e-learning modules for middle and high school students across the state of Nevada and beyond.

They sat through the remaining handful of students left to walk the stage, then watched as the graduating class threw their caps into the air, stripped out of the undoubtedly hot gowns, and scurried off like ants to whatever post-graduation festivities awaited them.

After kissing both men on the cheek prior to joining the ranks of her graduating peers, Lulu had promised she'd come by the next day to celebrate. But her plans today revolved around her group of friends, something Bo was 100 percent okay with. Unlike the bad apples she'd fallen in with at UC Berkeley, these were good people who lifted her up rather than dragged her down.

"So." Bo turned to Adam, joy swelling his heart. "What should we do to celebrate?"

Adam grinned. "I might have an idea."

"Oh? And what might that be?" Bo laughed when Adam's grin shifted to a mischievous smirk. "Uh-oh. Why do I have a bad feeling about this? No more surprises. You promised."

Over the years, Adam's unlucky streak had never faltered. But he loved surprises so much, he kept trying. Bo jokingly made him promise not to anymore after the last one found their kitchen half burnt to the ground, but he knew as well as Adam he hadn't meant it.

At least it'd resulted in an excuse to redecorate, and Adam had given him carte blanche and a blank check to do the kitchen—somewhere he frequented far more than Adam—any way he wanted it.

Rather than firing back with a stinger of his own, Adam twisted on the bench seat they shared and dropped to one knee. Amid a stadium full of people, he held up a Cartier jewelry box and bit his lip.

Bo's heart raced, and his stomach fell to his knees. He tried to get his mouth to close, but the dang thing hung open while Adam flipped the top of the box to reveal a gorgeous diamond-encrusted white gold—no, knowing Adam, *platinum*—engagement band.

Holy frickin' cow.

Butterflies burst free inside Bo's guts, their wings beating his innards until even his brain felt the impact. He grew light-headed and dizzy with delight.

Adam Littrell was proposing to him.

A horde of women to their right caught sight of Adam on his knee and swooned. Their excited squeals and eager pointing drew an even bigger crowd, and before Adam could get a word out, dozens of eyes watched their every move.

"I, ah, hadn't planned on an audience." Adam swallowed and glanced between the growing group of onlookers and Bo's undoubtedly goofy grin, his scruff-covered cheeks tinged with Bo's favorite shade of pink.

"What'd you think would happen if you did this in a giant group of humans following an emotional event?" Bo chuckled, and because he loved Adam more than words could possibly describe, he held out his left hand. "The answer to the question you haven't asked is an irrefutable yes. Now put that thing on my finger so I can further your embarrassment by kissing you brainless in front of all these people."

The little crowd cheered, drawing even more attention. As Adam fumbled to get the ring free—his cheeks now crimson but a grin splitting his face—someone in the throng recognized him. They sounded the alarm, and by the time Bo made good on his promise to plant a big, smacking kiss on Adam's lips, people were snapping pictures with their cell phones. Their special moment would be on the internet within seconds for all to see.

But Bo didn't care, and Adam wouldn't either. They were used to their private lives leaking into the public eye. It wasn't anything they sought, but when it happened, they accepted it and moved on.

Adam stood and pulled Bo into his arms. He pressed his lips close to Bo's ear, his warm breath tickling over the sensitive skin there. "My fuckin' surprises never pan out the way I'd planned. When will I ever learn?"

Bo nipped at Adam's jaw and laughed. He wouldn't change a thing about the man he loved, least of all his penchant for performing big, elaborate, and often epically failed surprises. If they were truly going to spend the rest of their lives together, he wanted him to be exactly who he was. Nothing more and nothing less. "I'm banking on never, baby, and I wouldn't have it any other way."

The End

A Note From the Author

I'd like to thank everyone, from the bottom of my writerly heart, who took the time to read Bo and Adam's story. As my debut novel, these characters are near and dear to me. Their publication was a bit of a rollercoaster, as my original publisher ran into an unfortunate financial crisis and my rights were reverted back to me after only two months in print, but I'm happy to say my boys found a home at Clandesdyne and I couldn't be happier.

If you enjoyed this first installment in my MM fairy-tale retelling series set in Las Vegas, Nevada, then keep your eyes peeled for the next book, which should be coming out around Winter 2020.

Finally, if you're interested in supporting authors such as myself, the best way to do so is to leave a review on Amazon, Goodreads, and/or the retailer of your choice. Reviews are the best way to help other readers find your favorite books and to thank the authors for putting their blood, sweat, and tears into the works you've enjoyed.

Until we meet again betwixt the pages of a book, go forth and be awesome, my lovelies.

Coming soon from Clandesdyne and Evie Drae....

*If you're looking for something with a bit more angst to
sink your readerly teeth into, look no further.*

*Landon has waited years for the freedom to love. Toby
just wants* freedom.

*That is, until their paths cross, and Toby discovers there's
more to the world than heartache and pain. If he can muster the courage to share the truth of his troubled past and
bleak future, Landon might just be the light in the dark he
never thought would come.*

Read on for a sneak peek of
He Owns My Heart,
*the multi-award winning first book in
Evie Drae's MM romance series,
Heart, Body, & Soul*

Chapter One

Landon stood outside a dilapidated motel off I-55 on the outskirts of Chicago. He held a rusted metal key, its edges dulled from years of use. The cracked red plastic of the keyring had the numbers 103 etched into its surface. A couple flecks of gold trapped in the sharp corners of the 1 and 3 were the only telltale sign the indented numbers used to bear a cheap inlay. His eyes drifted from the key in his hand to the chipped, robin's egg blue of the door bearing the same number.

On the other side of that worn, weathered piece of wood, a man waited for him. A man Landon had never met before, and a man he would never meet again.

Which was exactly how he wanted it... right?

Landon huffed out a breath and rolled his neck until it cracked, twice. "All right, asshole, you're the one who asked for this. Don't puss out now."

He nodded at his lackluster attempt at self-encouragement and took the few steps necessary to reach the door, jamming the key into the lock without allowing his body time to catch up to his mental reluctance.

When the door popped open, he swallowed to soothe a dry throat and walked into the dimly lit room. A single lamp positioned on the peeling laminate wood of the nightstand between two double beds threw an eerie copper glow into the space. Its flickering bulb did little to calm his raging nerves. He licked his lips and cast his gaze around the room, a mixture of relief and regret sinking heavily into his gut.

He was alone.

Landon eased the door shut and stood inside it, still gripping that damn key as if it held all the answers. What had he expected to find when he walked in here? A welcoming committee?

He nearly jumped out of his own flesh when a clunking bang broke the silence in tandem with the sound of water running. Landon's attention shifted to a door on the opposite side of the room as he ran a shaking hand through his long bangs, shoving them out of his face in the process. "Get a grip, Jenks. He's just using the john."

That phrase rattled through Landon's brain a moment before a bubble of hysterical laughter slipped past his lips. *Using the john.* Talk about an apropos inuendo. Wasn't a 'john' the term used for guys in Landon's current position? And wasn't he hoping to be just that.... *Used*?

The bathroom door clicked open, and Landon retreated a step as his mystery guest filled the frame, propping a shoulder against the warped wood. Black boxer briefs hugged his narrow hips and accentuated the cut of hard thighs. His chiseled, tanned chest was bare, his pec muscles flexing as he crossed his arms and committed further to his casual lean.

As Landon's hesitant gaze moved up, he bit back a slew of profanity threatening to tumble from his lips. If possible, the face attached to that Adonis body was even more beautiful. The jaw was strong and angular, dusted by a sandy five o'clock shadow a shade darker than the light brown of his hair, and a smile befitting an A-list model stretched a set of lush, full lips.

But it was those eyes that drew a low-grade whimper up Landon's throat. Their color wasn't distinguishable in the dim lighting, but they sparkled with humor and a hint of something else. Something darker, somehow tragic, yet hidden well behind a mask of cocky confidence.

Jesus fuck. What had he gotten himself into?

"Enjoying the view?"

Those words dripped into the silence like honeyed whiskey if it could make a sound. Smooth, deep, and sinful as hell.

"I...." Landon clenched his jaw. What was he supposed to say to that? Yes? "Ah...."

A chuckle rumbled up the Adonis's ripped chest, its warmth filling the stale air and sparking electricity over Landon's skin. "Am I making you nervous?"

"Ah, you could say that." Landon dropped his chin with a groan. "I'm sorry."

"No need to apologize." A hint of empathy softened the man's voice. "This your first time?"

Landon squeezed his eyes shut as heat crept up his throat, burning his cheeks. "That obvious, huh?"

That chuckle rolled through the room again, but this time it was closer. Landon peeked open an eye and drew back in surprise when his stare locked onto a pair of gorgeous hazel irises, perfectly on level with his own. The younger man—easily a decade if not more below Landon's own thirty-five years—ran a lazy hand through his sandy brown, styled-back locks before closing the distance between them even further.

"This your first time ever, first time with a guy, or just your first time with someone like me?"

Oh, God, oh, fuck. The flush kept climbing until the very tips of Landon's ears were aflame. "No, I mean, this isn't my *actual* first time. I-I've done it... I mean, *this*... before. I mean, shit, not *this*, but, you know... with a guy. Jesus. I'm sorry. I should just go."

The Adonis's radiant smile returned, nearly blinding Landon with its bright white brilliance. "You're adorable, you know that?"

Adorable. *Great.* Just what every guy wanted to be called when he stood in front of a nearly naked Greek god. A nearly naked Greek god he'd paid to have sex with him.

Shit.

Landon puffed out his cheeks on a heavy exhale. "I don't know what I'm doing here. This was a mistake. I should really go. I'm so sorry for wasting your time. I...." He scrunched up his face on a low groan. "Jesus, I'm sorry. I'm such an ass."

The man took a step back, offering a weak smirk. "I didn't mean to weird you out. I should be the one apologizing. I'm used to clients wanting that brash behavior. Didn't read the room right, I guess."

"It isn't your fault. I just...." Landon scraped his teeth over his lower lip and let out a shaky sigh. "This was a stupid idea. I don't know what I was thinking."

Quirking a brow, the guy folded those cut arms over his muscled chest, sending a ridiculous punch of lust straight into Landon's groin. "I assume you were thinking you'd get laid. That's what most of my clients are looking for. Nothing wrong with that."

"No, it wasn't...." Landon groaned and pressed a fist between his eyes. "I thought I could be something... some*one*... I'm not. Just for one night. But I can't. This isn't me. I don't do crazy shit like this."

When Landon glanced up, his heart squeezed. The younger man stood rigid, staring at the floor, his tongue running over that full bottom lip in a slow, repetitious rhythm. He looked about as lost as Landon felt, and wasn't that un-fucking-expected?

Then again, how else would he react to those harsh words? Landon had all but denounced his profession as something, what, beneath him? Idiot.

"I didn't mean to say there's anything wrong with doing this because there isn't. It just isn't something I've ever done or thought I'd do. I'm… boring. Non-adventurous. Not really the one-night-stand kinda guy, you know? Not that I'm saying this would be a one-night-stand. I mean, I know that's not what it means to you. Not that one-night-stands *mean* anything, I just…. Oh my God." He covered his face with both hands. "I'm having some sort of malfunction. Feel free to go and leave me alone to drown in my humiliation."

That spine-tingling laugh filled the room again. "Why don't we take this slow? We have all night, after all."

Landon let his hands fall even as his shoulders slumped with relief. Sure, he'd been the one to initiate this whole thing, but he was terrible at sex even when he was in an established relationship. How in the hell was he supposed to do it with a man he'd never met? A *professional*, even?

Maybe he could take things so slow they wouldn't happen at all?

Resolved to shift the awkward tension away from his sexual ineptitude, Landon cracked his knuckles. "Are you, ah, hungry by any chance?"

The Adonis tilted his head, a grin pulling at his lips. "I can always eat."

Landon yanked his cell free of his back pocket. "I saw a Chinese restaurant down the street advertising delivery. Does that… I mean… are you okay with that? We can do whatever. I just thought it'd be easiest."

"Chinese sounds amazing." His smile softened, treading carefully over Landon's disastrous nerves. "I'm happy with anything, but unfortunately, I don't carry money on jobs."

"Oh, yeah, no, of course. I've totally got this. Not a, ah, not a problem." Landon swallowed and ducked his head, cursing himself as he located the Chinese restaurant on his phone. "Do you know what you want, or—"

"I'm the opposite of picky. Just order two of whatever you're getting."

Landon nodded and turned away, putting the phone to his ear. He placed identical orders for beef and broccoli with fried rice and an egg roll on the side. At the last minute, he added a two liter of soda before giving the motel name and their room number. They took his card over the phone, then he hung up and shifted his gaze to the Greek god.

He'd slipped into a pair of black dress pants and a skintight ribbed tank in a dark charcoal gray. Part of Landon missed the delicious view, but a much bigger part of him appreciated the step away from painful awkwardness the clothing provided.

The Adonis tucked his hands into the front pockets of his slacks and rocked onto the balls of his bare feet. "So, food's en route. Wanna watch a little TV while we wait? Or did you have something else in mind? I'm down for whatever you wanna do, boss."

Landon glanced at the two double beds facing the old school tube television. "Yeah, no, ah, that sounds good. TV, I mean."

Nodding, the man wandered to the closest bed, snatching the remote off the nightstand with the flickering lamp before stretching out with his back propped against the cracked pleather headboard. He patted the bed beside him and cocked his lips into a lopsided grin. "Hop on board. Let's see what gems local television has to offer on a Saturday night."

Following the quiet directive, Landon slipped onto the bed. A scrumptious combination of sandalwood and leather drifted his direction, and Landon's cock twitched unhelpfully in his pants. He shifted, placing his folded hands over his lap and praying to achieve the level of nonchalance he aimed for.

As they skimmed through the slim selection of channels, Landon cleared his throat. "So…. Are you allowed to tell me your name?"

The guy lifted a careless shoulder. "Not something my clients usually wanna know, but I'm not against a first name exchange if you aren't." He offered a hand and Landon took it with a tentative squeeze. "Name's Toby."

Toby. The name suited his Adonis perfectly. A punch of fuck-yeah-that's-hot with a hint of cute to soften the blow. Landon pulled his hand back and re-crossed his arms. He was hesitant to share his own, but seeing as how he'd been the one to ask in the first place, it was only fair to offer his in return. "I'm Landon."

Toby's brow arched, and a crooked grin lifted one corner of his lips. "Landon, eh? Doesn't quite fit your adorable awkwardness. You sure you're not making that up?" When Landon's eyes widened and he opened his mouth to say God knows what in response, Toby winked. "Just kidding. It actually fits you quite well."

Adorable awkwardness. Jesus. He really had made an ass out of himself, hadn't he?

They landed on a local horror movie host who wore a theatrical vampire costume and spoke with exaggerated mouth movements and elongated vowels. Before the first scene of the B-movie flashed onto the screen, they'd shared several chuckles. When their food arrived a half hour later, Landon had to wipe tears of laughter from his eyes as he answered the door.

They ate their Chinese on the bed, sitting cross-legged, while they finished the ridiculous movie. By the time it was over, their food was gone, and Toby had mastered the host's outlandish, overdone speech pattern, drawing deep belly laughter from Landon each time he spoke.

He turned to Landon, and in that almost indiscernible, ridiculous cadence, he asked, "Would it be okay if I kissed you?"

Landon clutched his stomach as he came down off a rolling wave of laughter and swiped at his eyes. "I'm sorry, say what?"

This time, Toby spoke in his normal honeyed whiskey voice. A surprising intensity filled his eyes when their gazes met. "I said, would it be okay if I kissed you?"

The question threw a wrench into Landon's inner gears, and his brain stuttered to a halt. Hadn't there been a rule about not kissing? Even if there hadn't been, why would Toby want to kiss him after he'd made an ass of himself all evening? Snorting and crying in laughter was hardly better than stammering over the topic of sex like some adolescent virgin.

As if he could read minds, Toby traced a knuckle down the thick beard covering Landon's jaw. "I know you were told no kissing, but I'm allowed to revamp the rules on the fly if I want. And right now? I definitely wanna kiss you."

"Oh." Landon cursed the heat scorching his flesh, bringing a cold sweat to his brow.

"Does 'oh' mean yes or no?"

"Oh, ah…." A cackle rose up Landon's throat. He squeezed his eyes closed in horror. "God, I swear I'm not usually this awkward."

Toby's warm palm pressed against Landon's cheek. "Look at me."

Landon obeyed the gentle command, lifting his lids until his gaze fell on those soft golden-green eyes. Toby's countenance was no longer humored, filled instead with kindness and a sense of understanding Landon had never expected to find in a situation like this.

"All the stigma of being with a whore aside, is there any part of you that wants to see what might happen if I kiss you? Not because you paid me to, but because I want to. Because, maybe, you want to as well."

No way Toby really meant that. He undoubtedly had hot bodies throwing themselves at him left and right, not only because of his profession, but because he was exquisitely beautiful. No way he'd want someone like Landon.

Not unless he'd recognized him. And if he had, it wouldn't be Landon he'd want, would it? It'd be the man Landon had needed so badly to *not* be tonight.

That would be almost worse than not being wanted at all.

He'd paid for the illusion of being wanted. Of being needed. This show Toby put on was just part of the pricy package Landon had paid for to not only assure his anonymity, but to guarantee the happy ending he couldn't seem to find anywhere else.

What ever possessed him to believe this was a good idea? Why was he treating another human being like nothing more than a body to be used? Simply to slake his own needs and hide from his own failures?

He was such a piece of shit.

"Listen, I really should go. I, ah, I'll still pay you, of course, I just—"

Toby raised his other hand and cradled Landon's face with both palms, forcing Landon to make eye contact.

"You came here tonight for a reason. I'm not judging you, so stop judging yourself." The soft pads of Toby's thumbs brushed over Landon's lips. "Now, I'll ask you again…. What's 'oh' mean?"

About the Author

Evie Drae is a registered nurse by day and an award-winning male/male romance writer by night. She has won first place in seven Romance Writers of America® (RWA®) competitions, including the prestigious title "Best of the Best" in the 2018 Golden Opportunity Contest. She was a double finalist in the 2019 Golden Heart®, in both the Contemporary Romance and Romantic Suspense categories, and finished as a second-place runner-up in four additional RWA contests. As an added perk, she landed the fabulous literary agent Eva Scalzo from Speilburg Literary following a dual win in two separate categories of the 2018 Heart to Heart contest.

One of Evie's favorite things to do is encourage her fellow writers. To that end, she started the #writeLGBTQ, #promoLGBTQ, and #DailyWriteLGBTQ hashtags on Twitter to support and promote LGBTQ+ authors and allies while providing a safe space to connect and grow as a community. She is married to the love of her life, is the mother of two wonderful fur babies, and runs almost entirely on coffee and good vibes.

Evie loves to link up with fellow writers and readers. You can reach her directly at EvieDrae@gmail.com or find her on her social media accounts listed below. Twitter is where she's most active but be sure to check out her blog too. She focuses on reviews for LGBTQ+ authors and allies with the occasional quirky advice/recommendation post just to toss things up.

Website/Blog: https://www.eviedrae.com/
Twitter: https://twitter.com/eviedrae
Goodreads: https://www.goodreads.com/eviedrae
BookBub: https://www.bookbub.com/authors/evie-drae
Facebook: https://www.facebook.com/eviedrae
Instagram: https://www.instagram.com/eviedrae/
Pinterest: https://www.pinterest.com/eviedrae/

Printed in Great Britain
by Amazon

60019837R00130